RIVER RAPIDS

KATHY LEE

© Kathy Lee 2011
First published 2011
ISBN 978 1 84427 508 3

Scripture Union
207-209 Queensway, Bletchley, Milton Keynes, MK2 2EB
Email: info@scriptureunion.org.uk
Website: www.scriptureunion.org.uk

Scripture Union Australia
Locked Bag 2, Central Coast Business Centre, NSW 2252
Website: www.scriptureunion.org.au

Scripture Union USA
PO Box 987, Valley Forge, PA 19482
Website: www.scriptureunion.org

Scripture quotations are from the Contemporary English Version published by HarperCollins*Publishers* © 1991, 1992, 1995 American Bible Society.

British Library Cataloguing-in-Publication Data
A catalogue record of this book is available from the British Library.

Printed and bound by Nutech Print Services, India.

Cover design: Dodo Mammoth Reindeer Fox

✎ Scripture Union is an international charity working with churches in more than 130 countries, providing resources to bring the good news of Jesus Christ to children, young people and families and to encourage them to develop spiritually through the Bible and prayer.

As well as our network of volunteers, staff and associates who run holidays, church-based events and school Christian groups, we produce a wide range of publications and support those who use our resources through training programmes.

Chapter 1:

The river

Mallenford, my hometown, exists because of a river. Long ago, there must have been a ford – well, you can guess that from the name of the town. Then came the Old Bridge and the New Bridge, and the town grew up on both sides of the river.

I had to cross the Old Bridge every day to get to school. Sometimes I used to stop halfway over the bridge, looking down at the rushing water.

"What are the marks painted on that metal post?" I asked Mum, years ago.

"That's where the river level rose up to when it flooded," Mum said.

There were several marks. The highest one was only a couple of feet below the road. It had the date 1982 beside it.

"What? The water came right up to there? You're kidding."

"No, Maya, it really happened," said Mum. "It was lucky the bridge didn't collapse."

I was only about eight then, and I remember jumping up and down on the bridge a few times, seeing if it still felt strong. After all, it was more than 100 years old. But the pavement under my feet felt pretty solid.

In those days, I thought it would be great if the river flooded. What an idiot! Of course, I was just a kid. I had no idea what it would really be like.

But one day I found out.

★ ★ ★

It happened last winter, halfway through my first year at senior school.

Autumn had been a very wet one. Winter was even wetter, and by January the river was running high – not flooding, nothing like that, but whenever I crossed the bridge, I noticed how fast the water was flowing.

In Geography we had been looking at rivers. On a map, we saw where our river started out. It drained a huge area of hills and moorlands, the size of half the county. All the rain that fell anywhere inside that area would land up in our river, along with melting snow from the high hills.

We also talked about some of the other things that end up in rivers – farming chemicals, dirty water from drains, waste from factories…

"Dead rats," said one of the boys.

"Supermarket trolleys," said another.

"Diseases. Bacteria. Animal poo."

4

It was enough to make me wish I'd never gone swimming in the river during that hot summer a few years back.

"Another thing that we do to rivers," the geography teacher went on, "is try to change their behaviour. It's natural for rivers to flood sometimes. We talk about the 'flood plain' of a river, meaning the flat area where the water escapes to, if the river bursts its banks. Perhaps that only happens once in 100 years, so people forget what happened in their grandfather's time, and start building on the land. Then what happens?"

"Once in 100 years they get flooded out," said my friend, Evie.

"We're all right here, then," I said. "The last Mallenford flood was in 1982. We've got years and years before the next one."

"If only it was as predictable as that," said the teacher, and she started going on about climate change and all that stuff. Boring – I'd heard it all before. My mum is a bit of an eco-freak.

I gazed out of the window. It was raining again... pouring, in fact. I was going to get soaked going home. No good wishing Mum would come and pick me up. Apart from the fact that she couldn't leave the shop, we didn't have a car.

But I was lucky. After school, Evie's mum was waiting in her car. I got a lift nearly all the way home. She would have taken me right to the door, but she couldn't. There was a big sign, ROAD CLOSED, in front of the Old Bridge.

Evie's mum opened the car window and asked a policeman what was going on.

"The river level's rising," he said. "The Old Bridge may not be safe for vehicles. You'll have to go round by way of Market Street and the New Bridge."

"Are people still allowed to walk across?" I asked.

"At the moment they are."

"Don't worry. I can walk from here," I said to Evie's mum. "I'll be home in five minutes. Thanks for the lift!"

She looked relieved. She didn't want to make a long diversion to the other bridge. We had already gone past Evie's house which was on the south side of the bridge.

I got out of the car and started running. It might be only five minutes to my house, but that was enough to soak me to the skin. The rain was heavier than I could ever remember. The drains couldn't cope with it – water was actually coming up through the gratings.

As I hurried across the bridge, I took a quick glance at the river. The level was certainly high, but nowhere near that painted line marked 1982. What was all the fuss about?

We live in the flat above our shop. It's only 100 yards north of the bridge, but that's far enough to be a bit off the beaten track. The main shopping area is on the south side of the bridge. The row of shops on our side never seems very busy, and of course, it's worse on wet days.

As I went in, the shop bell clanged, and Mum looked up hopefully. She was disappointed to see it was only me, not a paying customer. Then she saw how wet I was.

"Oh, Maya! Take all those wet things off right now and have a hot bath. I'll close up in a minute. We're not going to get anyone coming in now."

"Too right. Did you know they're stopping people driving over the Old Bridge?"

Mum said, "All day, on the radio, they've been giving out weather warnings. There's been more rain today than we usually get in the whole of January. And most of it landed on you, I'd say. Go on, get upstairs and start running that bath."

As I lay in the bath, I could hear the rain beating on the roof like a never-ending drum roll. It was far louder than the usual bathroom noises – old pipes gurgling and water dripping from the leak in the roof. (Mum said we couldn't afford to get the leak fixed until the shop began to do a bit better.)

Water... water everywhere. I thought of it falling endlessly on moors and mountains, making marshland wetter and streams wider. And all that water would end up in our river. Maybe it would run higher than the record level painted beside the bridge.

Could the whole bridge get washed away? That would be quite exciting, I thought. Mallenford might even make the news on TV – which would be a first.

Like I said, the town existed because of the river. No one guessed that the river might try to destroy it.

Chapter 2:

Save what you can

"Maya! Wake up!"

I opened my eyes. It felt like the middle of the night, but my bedroom light was on, dazzling me.

"What time is it?" I said sleepily.

"Two o'clock."

"Two o'clock in the *morning*?"

"Come on, Maya. We're about to be flooded! Get up!"

"What?"

"The police were at the door. They said the river's burst its banks," Mum said. "Come on, get up. I need you to help me right now! We'll have to move stuff upstairs, out of the shop."

I got up and pulled on some clothes. Mum had gone scurrying downstairs, and I followed her more slowly, still not properly awake. Was this really happening, or was it a dream?

I stood aside to let Mum come up the narrow stairs. She was carrying a sack of beans.

"All the dried foods will be ruined if we get flooded," she said.

"But the river can't come up as far as this," I said. "It just can't."

"If you don't believe me, take a look outside," she called over her shoulder.

I unbolted the shop door and leaned out into the rain and the dark. Everything seemed normal except for the noise – a low roar like the sound of distant traffic. But it couldn't be traffic, not at 2am. Could it be the river?

As I gazed out, my eyes started getting used to the darkness. I saw the glimmer of street lights shining on water. Along by the pizza place, there was water right across the street! It wasn't a puddle. It was moving, rippling and eddying – the river was coming closer.

A door opened opposite us. Mr Brown, who owned the hardware shop, came out with his wife and baby. He hurried them into his car, along with a couple of suitcases.

"Mum, the Browns are leaving! Shouldn't we be getting out too?"

"Don't be silly. There's no need to panic," Mum said. "Shut that door and start helping me, girl."

Together, we carried some of the heaviest things up the stairs. In our small flat there was really no room for them. We stacked them up wherever we could – a barrel of olives beside the TV, a sack of wholemeal flour on the sofa.

"Mum, what about all the things in the stockroom?" I asked.

The stockroom was a small room at the back, not quite on ground level. You had to go up three steps from the shop. It was crammed full of boxes and bags that hadn't been opened yet. Mum said that the water wasn't going to reach that level – she hoped.

The shop floor was looking much emptier. A trail of spilt flour led up the stairs, but there wasn't time to bother about that. We looked out of the shop door for the last time.

Like the tide coming in, the edge of the water was getting closer. It had almost reached us. And that sound was louder now. Unmistakably, it was the sound of the river – the angry river, racing along, surging and swirling far beyond its banks.

I wondered if the Old Bridge was still there. There was no way of knowing. The bridge, or what was left of it, must be well under water by now.

"Don't you think we should get out of here?" I said to Mum.

"Where would we go?"

I hadn't thought of that. We had no car, and it was still pouring with rain out there. There were friends we might go to, but most of them lived on the other side of the river.

"I think we should stay," Mum said firmly. "If the ground floor gets flooded, we'll go upstairs."

"You don't want to leave the shop," I said.

"You're right, I don't. Everything we own is here. We have to do what we can to take care of it."

She started to stuff old bits of sacking between the doorstep and the bottom of the door. I didn't think they would keep the water out for long.

The shop floor was clear. Now we started emptying the lower shelves, scurrying around like ants from a nest that had been dug open. Tins and bottles, packets and jars, all got dumped upstairs wherever there was room for them.

By now, water was coming in under the door. A puddle spread quickly across the floor. It was cold on my bare toes, and Mum told me to put my boots on.

"That water could be filthy," she said. "It's safer not to touch it."

We had cleared most of the lower shelves. After my hundredth trip up and down the stairs, my legs were dying to have a rest. But Mum was still rushing around like a mad thing.

"The till! Empty the till," she said. "And we'd better unplug the fridges. Water and electricity – that's not a good mix."

"All the cold food will be ruined," I said, pulling out the plugs.

"Not just the food," she said. "The fridges will be ruined, if water gets into them."

"But Mum! We can't afford to buy new fridges!"

"The insurance will pay for them. At least I hope so."

I said, "If we're insured, why are we bothering to carry all that stuff upstairs?"

She stopped and stared at me. "That's a good question. I suppose I just felt... well, it's like an instinct, you know? Trying to save whatever you can."

"Stop, Mum. Sit down for a minute. You look done in."

But she wouldn't stop.

The water was getting deeper. Outside, it was swirling past the edge of the shop window. Inside, it was ankle deep and rising. And I was starting to feel scared.

"How deep is it going to get?"

"How would I know?" Mum snapped at me. "If you're not going to help, Maya, at least don't stand in the way."

"We should get out of here before it's too late," I said.

"It's already too late. It's not safe to go out there. Look how fast the water's moving – you'd be swept off your feet."

Water was rushing past the window, black under the street lights. It moved so fast that the postbox had a standing wave in front of it. And still the level was rising.

Mum must have seen the look on my face. "Don't worry, love. We'll be safe enough upstairs. It can't possibly come up as high as that."

I wanted to believe her, but she'd already been wrong once. She had told me the water wouldn't reach the stockroom – it was now up to the second step, and still climbing.

She said, "Why don't you go upstairs and put the kettle on? I could really do with a cup of tea. I'll be up in a minute."

"All right."

I switched on the 24-hour news channel as I waited for the kettle to boil.

"… And reports are coming in about serious flooding throughout the Mallen valley, from Tealbridge down to the coast. The flood waters are at their highest level since records began. At least two bridges have been destroyed, and the Met Office has issued a severe weather warning. The emergency services are advising people to stay indoors unless their journey is absolutely vital…"

So perhaps Mum was right. It was safer to stay here.

Now the camera showed a reporter with a flooded street behind him. In the darkness, it looked like a canal in Venice or somewhere, with water from wall to wall. And suddenly, I realised where it was – Mallenford High Street.

"Mum! Come and see this!"

The reporter said, "Here in Mallenford, dozens of homes have been evacuated. Many shops are flooded out, and the river level is still rising. It's believed that the Old Bridge, which had stood here since Victorian times, has been swept away by the floods. This is the deepest flooding that anyone here can remember. The worst thing is, it's still raining, with no sign of a let-up. The situation may get even worse before it gets better."

"Thank you, Tony." The news programme returned to the nice, dry studio and the smartly-dressed newsreader. "That was Tony Brigson in rain-soaked Mallenford. And now, the latest from the Australian Open…"

We never heard the latest from the Australian Open. It was cut off in mid-sentence as the TV went off, along with all the lights.

"Don't panic," said Mum. "It's only a power cut." She was trying to sound calm, but her voice was shaky.

The room was as black as a cave. The only sound was the deep roar of the river. I had never been so scared in my life.

Chapter 3:
Still raining

"Don't panic," Mum said again. "I know I've got some candles somewhere."

I could hear her stumbling around in the dark, tripping over stuff that wasn't normally there. The kitchen wasn't usually as dark as this – some light from the street lamps always came in through the blinds. But even the street lamps had gone out.

At last, she found some tea lights and a torch. She lit three of the little candles. It was amazing how their tiny flames held back the darkness.

"Mum, don't use up too many," I said. "It's still hours until daylight."

The electric kettle was useless now. We made some tea by boiling up water on the gas stove – at least that was still working. Before I'd drunk all of mine, I could feel my eyelids starting to close.

"Go back to bed, love," said Mum. "You need your sleep. I'll wake you up if – "

"If what? If my bed starts floating away?"

All at once we heard a crash from downstairs.

"What was that?" I gasped.

"The window caving in, I expect," said Mum. "All that water pressing against the glass... I didn't think it would stand up to it for long. You have to remember..." She stopped suddenly.

Whenever something went wrong with the shop or the flat – leaks in the roof, cold draughts, rotting floorboards – she used to say, "You have to remember this is an old building." But she didn't say it this time. Was she worried that the whole building would get swept away? Which was stronger, the building or the river?

She shone the torch down the stairs, trying to see into the shop. The water had suddenly risen much higher – almost half-way up the stairs. It was like a dark pool edged with a scum of grey foam.

Everything in the stockroom must be getting soaked, and all the things that were left on the shelves of the shop. I hoped Mum was right about the insurance paying for it. If not, we would never find the money to start up again.

I picked my way between the piles of packets and jars, trying to get to the front window. But when I looked out, there was nothing to see. No street lights, no lighted windows – only darkness. Nothing to hear except water rushing by, and rain beating against the glass.

It felt as if the whole town had vanished, wiped off the map. I knew that couldn't really be true. There were other buildings out there, and probably other people trapped like us. But we couldn't see them or talk to them. We were like the last two people alive.

Suddenly, I remembered my phone. I texted Evie – I didn't call her in case she was still asleep. There was no way of knowing if the floods had reached her house on the far side of the river.

She called me back straight away.

"Maya! Are you OK? Where are you?"

"Still at home. The whole shop's flooded out – we're upstairs. What about you?"

"Our place got flooded too. We're in the school hall. There's about a hundred people here, and it's total chaos."

"Yes, I can hear." There was a babble of voices in the background and a child crying.

"The police came and told us to get out of the house," Evie said. "Didn't they warn you?"

"They did, but Mum didn't want to leave the shop. And now it's too late. We can't leave – we're stuck here."

Mum called out, "That's right, it's all Mum's fault as usual," loud enough for Evie to hear. She laughed.

"I wish we had stayed at home," she said. "Nobody seems to know what's going on here. And there's no food, no beds, nothing. It's like a disaster movie without the film stars."

My phone battery was running low. I'd better be careful – without a power supply, I wouldn't be able to recharge it. I said goodbye to Evie, feeling a bit better than before... a bit less lonely.

If only it wasn't so dark! I asked Mum how long it would be until daylight.

"Another three hours, at least," she said. "Why don't you go back to bed and try to get some sleep?"

"Are *you* going back to bed?"

"No. I can't even if I wanted to. My bed's buried under lentils and chick peas."

I knew the real reason she wasn't going to sleep. She was keeping watch on the water level. If it reached us, what would we do – climb up into the attic?

I watched her ferreting around in her desk. She was sorting out papers and shoving them into a bag. Then she disconnected the computer and hid it in the loft. She was doing the same as before – getting ready to save what she could.

I should be helping her. *In a minute... just give me a minute...*

Then I fell asleep.

★ ★ ★

When I woke up, I couldn't think where I was. The window was in the wrong place, and my bed felt odd... no, not the bed, it was the sofa... and what was that sack of flour doing there?

Suddenly, I remembered. The floods!

I sat up in a panic, looking around for Mum. But it was all right. She was slumped in the armchair, fast asleep, snoring quietly.

I could see daylight outside the window, so I went to look out. The street was still awash with water. It looked quite deep – almost up to the top of the post box outside.

It was the same at the back. Our small yard was completely flooded, and so was the narrow alley beyond, although here the water wasn't moving as fast as in the street. Maybe it would be possible to fight your way through it without getting swept away.

But where would you go? The nearest high ground was over half a mile away. Everything from here to Mar Hill was under water. And it was still raining. Black clouds hung over the town like an evil threat.

Indoors, the flat looked a total mess, with piles of stuff everywhere. At least we wouldn't starve to death – we had enough to feed us for several years, although we might get sick of brown rice and organic pumpkin seeds.

Opening the door at the top of the stairs, I checked the water level in the shop. It didn't seem to have got any deeper since last night. It was a murky brown colour, lapping gently against the seventh step down. I knew there were 13 steps altogether, so if I was mad enough to go downstairs, my head would still be above water. But as Mum had said, the water was probably filthy. Not to mention freezing cold.

Mum was still asleep. She looked worn out.

I put some bread in the toaster, forgetting that the power was off. After a while I took it out and tried to toast it on the grill of the cooker. But I couldn't get the gas to light. Maybe the gas supply had been cut, too.

So I had a cold breakfast. The air in the flat felt quite chilly. I put my jacket on, but it didn't help much. If we were stuck here for days and days, how would we manage to keep warm?

The worst thing was having no TV and no computer. My phone was pretty basic – it didn't have the Internet, and anyway I mustn't waste what was left of the battery. But I was desperate to hear the news, to find out what was going on.

I texted Evie again, but she didn't answer. It was only 7.45 – she might be asleep, if anyone could sleep in the school hall with dozens of other people.

I went back to the window, hoping to see some signs of life. But nothing was moving outside – only the water and the rubbish that was floating along. Broken branches, a farm gate, an oil drum, all went bobbing and dancing past my window.

And then I saw the girl.

She was clinging onto a sort of raft, or maybe a bit of broken fence. Only her head and arms were above the water. She looked absolutely terrified as the river swept her towards me.

"Mum!" I yelled.

In another minute it would be too late to do anything. The flood would carry the girl away.

"Mum! Quick! Help me!"

She jolted awake. "What's going on?"

I opened the window, looking around frantically for a rope or something to throw. Then I saw the long pole we used for opening the trapdoor to the loft. But would it reach?

I stretched as far as I could, reaching out with the pole. The hook on the end caught the edge of the fence panel. Mum grabbed me from behind, just in time to save me from being dragged out of the window.

Between us we pulled the raft closer to the wall. The water wasn't running so swiftly there, and we were able to hold it steady. But it was six feet below us. There was no way we could lift the girl up.

And she didn't look as if she had any strength left. She was soaking wet and shaking with cold. I took in the fact that she looked Chinese. She gazed up at us with frightened eyes.

"Hold on tight," Mum said to me. "I'll go downstairs and get her in through the shop window."

"No, you can't! It's not safe!"

But I couldn't stop her. She went down the stairs, and I heard her cry out as she stepped into the cold water. That didn't stop her either.

Suddenly, I realised what a risk she was taking. She couldn't even swim properly.

I gripped the pole as hard as I could, fighting the strength of the river. I knew I couldn't hold it for much longer.

Oh, come back, Mum... please come back...

Chapter 4:

Rescued

"Maya, can you hear me?" Mum called up from below.

"Yes!"

"I'm going to pull the raft into the shop. Unhook the pole, can you?"

For one desperate moment I thought I couldn't unhook it. Then it came free, and I lurched backwards. I looked out, just in time to see the raft disappearing. Mum must have dragged it through the broken shop window.

I ran to the stairs and went down far enough to see into the shop. Oh, that water was cold! But at least it wasn't moving. The shop was like a safe harbour, much calmer than the river outside.

Mum was shoulder-deep in water. She pulled the raft towards the stairs, talking to the girl all the time.

"You'll be OK, love. You're safe now. We'll get you upstairs and dry you out, all right?"

I don't know if the girl understood what Mum was saying. Drenched and shivering, she looked ready to collapse. It took all our strength to get her up the stairs.

"We'll put her in a warm bath to heat her up," Mum said to me.

"Is there any hot water?"

"I don't know! Run the tap and find out. Come on, we don't want her to die of cold!"

Even with the power off, there was still some heat left in the tank. I ran all the warm water into the bath. We took off the girl's outer clothes – she tried to stop us but didn't have the strength. Then, between us, we lifted her in.

She lay there like a bit of seaweed washed up on a beach. She didn't speak, and she still looked very frightened.

"It's all right, love, you're safe now," said Mum.

The girl didn't react at all. Maybe she couldn't speak English. She definitely looked Chinese, or maybe Japanese. That was odd – there weren't many Chinese people living in Mallenford, and it wasn't the sort of place where tourists came.

"She looks like she should be in hospital," I said. "But how is an ambulance going to get here?"

"I don't know. But you're right – she needs help. I'm going to ring 999."

Mum went into the kitchen to use her mobile phone. When she came back, she said, "They're going to try to get a boat here. But it might take a while."

I realised that Mum was shivering. She was almost as wet as the girl was. I wasn't too bad – I had only gone in as far as my knees.

"Mum, go and get changed," I said. "I'll keep an eye on her."

The girl's eyes were closing. I didn't know much about first aid, but I had an idea that you should try to keep people talking, to make sure they stayed conscious. When I touched her on the shoulder, she leapt awake and sort of flinched away from me.

"I'm not going to hurt you," I said, keeping my voice as gentle as I could. Maybe she would understand the tone of it, even if the words meant nothing. "What's your name?"

She whispered something that sounded like Leanne, or maybe Li An.

"Hi," I said. "I'm Maya. Where are you from?"

But she didn't answer.

At first, I'd thought she was about the same age as me – she was about my height, and very thin – but I was starting to change my mind. She could be 14 or 15. Her clothes, lying on the floor, looked like charity shop rejects – faded T-shirt, old grey jogging bottoms, no shoes.

I couldn't begin to guess where she had come from. She might have been carried downriver for quite a long way, from the far side of town, or even from Tealbridge, several miles away. But before that, where in the world was she from? Somewhere far to the east, was all I could say for certain.

She didn't seem to like me looking at her, so I turned away. I caught sight of my own reflection in the mirror. My face is a bit of a mystery. People sometimes ask me if I'm part Chinese, or Malaysian, or Thai. My eyes are sort of almond-shaped. My skin colour is golden brown and my hair is reddish-brown and curly.

I am obviously a mixture of different nationalities. But what went into the mixture? It's no good asking Mum, because she's not my birth mother. She adopted me when I was a few months old. I was abandoned as a baby – left in a toilet at Euston Station. Probably I'll never find out who my parents were, but most of the time it doesn't bother me. Mum has been a good mother to me, and I never missed having a dad.

Now and then, I think it would be nice to know a bit more about myself. Perhaps, when I'm 18, I'll try to find out what I can. Perhaps I'll never know more than I do now.

★ ★ ★

Mum came bustling back. She felt the temperature of the bath-water, which wasn't very warm by now. It was time to get the mystery girl out of the bath.

"Up you get, love."

We helped the girl out. Mum wrapped her in a big towel and dried her like a baby. I found some clothes of mine which might fit her, and some dry underwear.

It was a bit like dressing a doll. The girl didn't try to stop us putting the clothes on her, but she didn't help, either. Mum said she was in a state of shock.

Just as we finished getting her dressed, there was a shout from outside. I went to the front window. There was a boat outside, with three people in it. The motor was working hard to keep it still against the current.

"Is this the place? Did you phone for medical help?" asked a young woman in bright orange waterproofs.

"Yes. We've got a girl who nearly drowned. My mum rescued her."

I wondered how the woman was going to get in. Would she wade through the water into the shop? She solved the problem by throwing us a rope ladder, which we tied to the window-frame.

Five minutes later, the mystery girl was being helped down the ladder into the boat. She still hadn't said more than those two sounds which might be her name.

There was room in the boat for Mum and me. At first I thought Mum would refuse to go. But she sighed and said we might as well leave. Things were only going to get worse if we stayed.

She picked up the bag she'd packed earlier, with all our money and vital papers inside. I snatched up a few belongings – my phone and its charger, my make-up bag, my favourite top – and stuffed them into the bag. We climbed down the ladder, which shook alarmingly, and sat down in the boat.

It was still raining. The boat swung round in a wide arc, heading up the street away from the river. I knew it was taking us away from our home and everything we owned. I waved a silent goodbye to it all.

What would happen when the floods went down? Anyone could walk right into our shop through the broken window. They could go upstairs and take whatever they wanted... if any of it was worth taking.

No good worrying about that now. There was nothing we could do.

Reaching shallow water, we had to get out of the boat and wade to where an ambulance stood waiting. One of the paramedics tried to help the girl, but she kept pushing their hands away. She looked terrified. She was eventually lifted onto a stretcher and carried to the ambulance.

"Where will you take her?" Mum asked another paramedics.

"Not Mallenford hospital, that's for sure," he said. "We can't get there – both the bridges are down. I expect it will be Tealbridge. Is the girl a relative of yours?"

"No. We just saw her in the water and pulled her out," I said. "We don't know anything about her."

"I don't think she speaks much English," Mum said, looking anxious.

"Don't you worry, love. We'll take care of her."

The ambulance drove away, splashing through the puddles.

"Now what?" I asked Mum. "What are we supposed to do?"

Chapter 5:

Disaster victims

We had nowhere to go. We had nothing, except the clothes we were wearing and the things in Mum's bag. And it was still pouring with rain.

The boat had gone off on another medical call-out, leaving us alone except for a TV crew setting up some equipment. We wouldn't normally have bothered them, but there was no one else to ask.

"Excuse me, do you know where people are being taken to when they get evacuated?" Mum said.

"I think it's a school," said a man I vaguely recognised. Oh yes – I'd seen him on TV, reporting about the floods.

"But we can't get to Mallenford School," I said. "It's over the river."

"No, another school on this side," said a woman. She looked at some papers pinned to a clipboard. "Actually it's a nursery. The Green Lane Nursery – we did a couple of interviews there."

"Oh, I know where that is," said Mum, and we turned to go.

"Wait a minute. How would you feel about being interviewed?"

"I'd rather not," said Mum.

"I'll do it," I said eagerly. I had always wanted to be on TV.

They stuck me in front of a camera, soaking wet as I was, with rain dripping off my nose. I didn't even get the chance to comb my hair. The reporter talked to me as if I was about five years old.

"Were you very frightened when the floods surrounded you?"

No, I loved every minute, I wanted to say.

"Yes, quite frightened," I heard myself say. "And it was cold, and all the power went off."

"And then you were rescued by boat! Was it exciting?"

"Not as exciting as when my mum rescued this girl…"

The camera swung towards Mum, and she had to tell the whole story. She looked totally embarrassed. Later, when we watched the TV news, Mum was on it and I wasn't. I'd missed what was probably my only chance of being famous.

The TV crew did help us, though. The woman with the clipboard got us a lift in a smart-looking car. The driver didn't look too pleased when we got in, making damp marks on his seats. But he took us to the Green Lane Nursery, where we were given a hot drink and some dry clothes.

The clothes weren't great – a pink and yellow spotted top, jeans that were too big for me, and purple trainers.

"Just put them on and don't complain," said Mum. "Who's going to see you?"

"All those people out there."

"Well, they're all in the same state as us. It's an emergency, not a fashion show."

There were dozens of people there already – old people, families, and a couple of girls I knew. Most people were sitting around chatting, or watching the TV news. There wasn't much else to do, unless you felt like playing with the doll's house or the train set.

I talked to Joss and Amelia, who were in my year at school.

"What's going to happen to us?" I asked, but neither of them knew.

"We can't sleep here tonight," said Joss. "The only bed is in the Wendy House."

"I think they're trying to find us beds for the night in people's homes," said Amelia.

Joss said, "One good thing, they can't make us go to school. Not until the bridges are rebuilt, and my dad says that could take months."

Amelia looked alarmed. "We can't stay off school for months! We'd get behind with our work. And I'd be bored to death. Maybe they'll send us to a different school on this side of the river."

Amelia is quite clever – or she likes to think she is. Once we had to write about our ideal job. Most people said things like "fashion model" or "racing driver". Amelia wrote "Prime Minister."

"Oh, look. The rain's stopped," said Joss.

"Don't get too excited. It will take ages for the floods to go down," Amelia said. "And even then we won't be able to go home straight away."

"Why not?" I asked.

"Because everywhere will be in such a mess. Houses uninhabitable. Furniture ruined. Haven't you ever seen it on TV?"

"Yeah, I've seen it, but I never thought it would happen to me," said Joss.

I knew what she meant. Disasters were things that happened to other people in far-away countries. Not here – not in Mallenford.

★ ★ ★

At lunchtime we were given a free meal provided by the local burger bar. Mum is normally quite fussy about what she eats. She likes organic, fair-trade, low cholesterol, healthy stuff – not bacon cheeseburgers and fries. But that day she ate what she was given, without a word.

I was learning what it felt like to be a disaster victim. The worst thing was the feeling of helplessness. You couldn't decide things for yourself. You had to eat, drink and wear whatever you were given, and be grateful.

In the late afternoon, an announcement was made. The floods seemed to have stopped rising. If there was no more rain, the river should gradually go back to its usual level, but that might take several days. Meanwhile, many people had offered to take in flood victims until they were able to go home again.

Mum and I were given an address to go to: 11 Valley Road. It was only a few streets away. We gathered up our few belongings and went there straight away.

It felt weird to be ringing a stranger's doorbell, asking for shelter. But Mr and Mrs Robertson were very nice.

"Come in, come in. You must be dying for a cup of tea! I'm June, and this is Vince."

June was plump and smiley; Vince was lean and grey-haired. Their house had an old-fashioned look, with lace curtains, flowery carpets, and a china cat on the windowsill. It was far enough from the river to feel safe from flooding. Sitting on the sofa, having tea and home-made cake, I felt in a different world.

We had to tell our story all over again.

"Oh, how awful," June said. "And that poor girl – I wonder what happened to her?"

"Maybe I could ring the hospital in Tealbridge," said Mum.

"Use our phone," said Vince. "Go on, feel free."

So Mum rang the hospital, but they couldn't tell her anything, as she wasn't a relative and didn't even know the girl's name.

"They sounded a bit disorganised," said Mum, putting the phone down. "I expect they had quite a lot of emergency cases coming in today."

"It was on the radio about a woman who had a baby in a flooded house," said Vince. "And an old man had a heart attack – the ambulance-boat took ages to reach him. We don't realise how much we depend on roads and bridges and things."

June took us upstairs and showed us the room we would be sleeping in. It had belonged to her daughter Laura, who was living in London. On the walls there were posters of boy bands from years ago.

Mum would sleep in the single bed; I would have a camp bed on the floor. "I'm sorry I can't give you a proper bed," June said to me.

"This is fine," I said, because the room looked a lot more comfortable than the Wendy House at the nursery.

"It's really kind of you to take us in," said Mum. "I don't know how to thank you."

Downstairs, the front door slammed.

"That will be Dylan," said June. "He's been out with his camera taking pictures of the floods. I hope he hasn't got soaked."

She hurried off to take care of Dylan, whoever he was. June was obviously someone who liked taking care of people... which was a good thing for us.

Later that evening, I discovered that Dylan was a boy I vaguely knew. He was in the year above me. He'd once given a talk in Assembly about the ghost stories of Mallenford. Everyone thought he was a bit strange – I mean, who would choose to give a talk in school if they didn't have to?

June and Vince looked too old to be his parents. Also, he called them by their first names.

"Is Dylan your grandson?" I asked June. Mum and I were helping her to wash up after supper.

"We're his foster carers," said June. "He's been with us for several years. He's a nice lad."

A nice lad... maybe, but hadn't she noticed that he was kind of odd?

Crossing the room, I almost tripped over the jeans I was wearing, which were much too long. June looked me up and down. Perhaps she thought I looked kind of odd too.

She said, "Maya, if you want to have a rummage through the drawers upstairs, you might find some clothes of Laura's that would fit you. They could be a bit out of fashion, though."

"They can't be worse than what I'm wearing now," I said.

I went to bed wearing Laura's striped pyjamas. I couldn't believe it was less than 24 hours since the flooding began. So much had happened in one day!

Then I heard a sound I dreaded... the patter of raindrops on the window. And I knew that our problems weren't over yet.

Chapter 6:
Kindness to strangers

Next day, it was still raining, but not a downpour like Monday's. The TV news showed a helicopter view of Mallenford, still badly flooded. I thought I could make out the roof of our place, but before I could be certain, the helicopter had moved on.

"Over a thousand people have been evacuated from their homes," the newsreader was saying. "Most are staying in temporary accommodation. Some people have tried to return home, but police have cordoned off the flooded area because it is still unsafe. The river level appears to be falling slowly, but with more rain, it could rise again."

"Oh, great," I said.

"It could be worse," said Mum. "At least nobody got killed."

"There is still no news of a man believed to have been swept downriver when a bridge collapsed," the newsreader went on. "He was returning home in the early hours after celebrating a friend's birthday. Police stopped him as he was about to cross the New Bridge in Mallenford. But he refused to listen to their warnings. He jumped over a barrier, and before he reached the other side, the bridge was carried away by the flood waters."

"Wrong, Mum. Somebody did get killed," I said.

"Shhh," said Mum. "I'm trying to watch this."

The news report went on for ages. It showed flooded houses, half-submerged cars, and roads that led nowhere except into the river. Everything looked grey – grey river, grey sky, grey town.

"This is so depressing," I said. "It doesn't look like Mallenford will ever be the same again."

I went upstairs to ring Evie – my phone was recharged by now. She sounded depressed too.

"We're staying at my cousins' house," she said. "There isn't really room for all of us. I had to sleep on the living-room sofa, and my little brat of a cousin came in and started jumping all over me before I was awake. And we might have to live here for days – or even weeks! I can't stand it!"

"Sounds terrible," I said.

"It is. Where are you now?"

"At Dylan Harvey's house. You know, Dylan in Year 8? The guy who's into ghosts and mysteries and all that?"

"Oh yeah, I know. He's all right looking, isn't he?" She giggled.

I thought about this. It was true, Dylan looked all right – dark hair, dark eyes, quite tall. But there was something kind of secretive about him, as if he knew more than he would ever tell you. I wondered why he was living with foster carers instead of his own family.

When I went downstairs, Dylan said to me, "Want to see my video of the floods?"

"Go on then."

He took me outside, to a sort of shed which he called his base. It was rather cold and draughty. Raindrops rattled on the metal roof.

Dylan had a computer in there, along with a games console, a dartboard, and a biscuit tin full of snacks. He offered me some Doritos. "I have to keep them in a tin or the mice nibble them," he said.

"Mice! I hate mice!"

"Don't worry. They won't show themselves in daylight."

Feeling rather nervous, I waited while Dylan connected his video camera to the computer. Then he replayed the video he'd taken the previous day. I was quite impressed – he'd managed to film some places the TV crews had never reached. A flight of steps that looked more like a waterfall... a boat trapped in a flooded tree... water racing beneath the arches of a bridge...

"Where is that?" I asked. "I thought both the bridges had been destroyed."

"That's the old railway bridge. It was still standing when I filmed that. I was walking away when I heard this noise – a rumbling noise, like an avalanche or

41

something. And the bridge just sort of crumbled into the river. I wish I'd got it on film!"

I said, "Mallenford's going to be so weird without the bridges."

The two halves of Mallenford were cut off from each other now. The only way to get to school, or the cinema, or Evie's house, would be a long detour through Tealbridge and back again.

"I suppose people could wade across the river," Dylan said.

"In summer, maybe. It's shallower in summer. But if you tried it in winter, you'd get washed right down to the sea."

"Lunch is ready," June called from the back door, and we hurried in through the rain.

That was one good thing about staying here – the food was great, although June kept on apologising for it.

"I've had to get the old bread maker out and bake some bread. The local shop's completely out of bread and milk, and lots of other things, too. I suppose people are panic-buying, and the delivery vans can't get through."

"Your home-made bread is delicious," said Mum.

"What will happen," I asked, "if the shop runs out of food?"

June said, "They won't run out completely. Not if people are sensible. They said they've got an extra delivery coming tomorrow, if the floods go down a bit."

"Don't worry, June won't let anybody starve," said Dylan.

★ ★ ★

By the next day, the floods were slowly receding. But still the town centre was cordoned off by the police.

Mum and I went as close as we could to the taped-off part of the High Street. We could see our shop front not far away. Shallow water was lapping at the doorstep. There was a brown, muddy tidemark along the whole street at shoulder level.

I really wanted to go home, and I could tell that Mum felt the same. Even though June and Vince were nice, we were visitors in their house. It wasn't like being in our own place.

But there had been warnings on TV about going back too soon. The flooded river had been contaminated with water from the sewers. All buildings would need to be disinfected and dried out before anyone could go back to live there.

Mum had called the insurance company. It took her a long time to get through to them – dozens of other people were ringing up. They said someone would need to come and inspect our shop before they could pay out any money.

So we couldn't afford to go to a hotel or a bed and breakfast place. We would have to stay at Dylan's house.

"You stay as long as you like, love," June said. "It's no trouble."

"Are you sure? It's costing you money, feeding us," said Mum. "I can't even pay you back. But I will, when the insurance money comes through."

Vince told her not to worry.

I said to Dylan, "Vince and June are being really good to us. I mean, it's not like we're family or anything. We've never even met them before. Why are they doing it?"

"Look over there, if you want a clue," said Dylan.

He was pointing at a poster on the kitchen wall. It showed a refugee mother with her baby. She was dressed in rags, and looked as if she was starving. The words underneath said:

I was hungry and you gave me food.
I was thirsty and you gave me drink.
I was a stranger and you took me in.
I was naked and you clothed me.
I was sick and you visited me.
I was in prison and you came to me…
Whatever you did to the least of my brothers, you
did to me.

I understood the first part plainly enough, but what did the last line mean? I asked Mum about it later.

"I think it's a quote from the Bible," she said. "I'm not sure."

Mum knew quite a lot about various religions. In the shop she had books on everything, from Buddhism to Zoroastrianism – everything, except Christianity.

"So, are June and Vince Christians, then?" I asked.

"I suppose so. We were strangers and they took us in… and if there were more people who behaved like that, the world would be a better place." She sighed, and laid out my sleeping bag. "Come on now, Maya. Time for bed."

Chapter 7:

A disaster

"This is so unfair," Joss moaned. "It's an emergency! They shouldn't be making us go to school!"

"You can't exactly call it an emergency. Not now," said Amelia. "It's not like anyone's life is in danger."

"What would you call it, then?"

"A crisis... a predicament... an unfortunate event," Amelia said, looking pleased with herself.

"A disaster," said Joss.

"Hardly a disaster," said Amelia.

Joss said, "It's a disaster having to go to Tealbridge School."

"What's wrong with Tealbridge School?" I asked.

"It's full of people from Tealbridge. They're all morons."

A week had gone by. The river was still running high, but it was back in its normal course – normal, except that the bridges had disappeared. All you could see of the Old Bridge was a disturbance in the river, where water swirled around the broken bridge supports. The metal post showing the flood levels was visible, but if the latest level was to be added, a taller post would be needed. No one had ever expected so terrible a flood.

46

A temporary replacement bridge was going to be built, but that could take months. Until it was ready, people from our side of Mallenford were being sent to school in Tealbridge. We were waiting for the bus that would take us there.

Looking around, I saw that there weren't many people from my year. Most of my friends lived on the south side of the river. Joss and Amelia were all right, but they weren't what I'd call real friends. I had walked to the bus stop with Dylan, but then he met up with a mate of his from Year 8. I felt quite lonely, and wished Evie was there.

At Tealbridge, things got worse. Joss, Amelia and I were all put in different classes. From now on we were on our own.

Tealbridge School didn't seem to have a uniform, except for a black sweatshirt. I was wearing Laura Robertson's old school clothes – white shirt, green skirt and jumper. I had refused to wear the tie that went with them, but I still felt far too dressed up, like the Queen at a football match. And it was plain that I was an outsider. I didn't belong.

No one in my new class made any effort to be friendly. People stared at me and whispered to each other. I thought it was just because I was new. But then I heard a couple of things that sounded quite racist.

That came as a shock. It had never happened at Mallenford School, even though most people there were white and I wasn't. But then I'd grown up with them. They knew me as a person: Maya Grant, not bad-looking, quite sporty, a bit of a laugh. They were used to the way I looked, and they never called me names like these girls did. I was hearing the words "foreign rubbish"... "dumb Chinky"... "flied lice"... and a few much nastier things that I won't write down.

At first I did my best to ignore the whispers. I kept away from the group of girls who were talking about me. But then, at the end of the day, when I was trying to find my way out of the school, they suddenly appeared in front of me. Their faces were full of hate.

"What are you doing here?" one of them asked.

"Yeah, why don't you go back where you came from?" demanded another. "Foreign muck!"

"Get out of here, Chinky!"

Someone shoved me against the wall – not hard, but I could tell that this was just the beginning. I felt quite frightened. We were near the cloakrooms, in a shadowy corridor, with no adults in sight.

Looking around frantically, I spotted Joss and Amelia. I pushed my way between two of the girls and headed towards them. I had never been so pleased to see them.

"What was all that about?" Joss asked.

"Nothing," I said rather shakily. "They were just being stupid."

48

For some reason, I didn't want to tell them the details, especially when they both seemed to have had a good day. Joss had met a boy she liked the look of. Amelia had written a poem which the English teacher read out to the whole class. They had both decided that Tealbridge wasn't going to be so bad after all.

I didn't tell Mum about it either. She had enough to worry about with the shop. An insurance man had looked at the place and told her how much the insurance company would pay out. He said the shop had been under-insured. The insurance wouldn't pay for everything that needed to be done – repairs and redecorating, replacing the fridges, buying new stock.

"What are we going to do, then?" I asked.

"I'm not sure. Maybe I should sell the shop and try to get a job somewhere."

Mum sounded depressed. Having her own shop had been her dream ever since I could remember. She'd been able to make it a reality two years ago, when her aunt died and left her some money.

Maybe the dream was over now. Was that a good thing? An office job, like she used to have, would be a lot less worry than the shop… but much more boring.

"The trouble is, I might not be able to sell the place," she said. "There are going to be quite a few shops on sale in Mallenford pretty soon. I was talking to the Browns from the hardware shop – they're closing down.

They don't think it's worth the effort of getting going again. Same with the bookshop."

I suddenly realised that if the shop was sold, our home above it would go too. "But Mum! Where would we live?"

"I don't know. We'll have to think quite hard about this. Maybe we should move somewhere else. The Browns are moving up north."

"I don't want to move up north!"

"Don't panic. We'll be here for quite a while longer. Whatever happens, I have to get the shop sorted out."

★ ★ ★

Next day, I decided not to wear the green uniform. In a drawer, I found a black top that didn't look too different from the Tealbridge School uniform. But it wasn't really the clothes that made me an outsider. It was my face – and there was nothing I could do about that.

For a day or two, nothing much happened. There were a few more whispers and stares from those girls. A plump, greasy-haired girl called Matilda was the worst one. She stuck her big foot out in front of me whenever I passed her, trying to trip me up. I soon learned to avoid her, which wasn't difficult, for she stood out like a hippo in a herd of deer.

Normally, I would have tried to speak to other people and make friends. But I didn't want to risk getting picked on again, so I kept my head down and got on with my work. At lunchtime and break I always met up with Joss and Amelia. I knew that Matilda and her friends wouldn't have a go at all three of us.

On Friday morning, Amelia wasn't at the bus stop – Joss said she was off sick. Joss was excited because there was going to be a lunchtime disco for Year 7 to raise money for the new gym. Kieran, the boy she liked, had asked her if she was going.

"Are you coming, Maya?" she asked me. "It's a quid to get in, but it should be a laugh."

"Yeah, I suppose so."

She didn't notice that I was depressed. She rabbited on about Kieran all the way to Tealbridge.

At lunchtime, Joss couldn't wait to get to the disco, which was held in the school hall. Outside the door was a group of girls collecting the entrance money. Oh-oh... I recognised most of them, including Matilda.

I hung back, letting Joss go in first. I was hoping they wouldn't notice me. Avoiding their eyes, I handed over my money. Matilda snatched it.

Then she stepped in front of me, barring my way. She said, "You can't come in."

"Why not?" I said angrily.

"Because it costs a pound."

"I already gave you the money!"

"No you didn't."

"Yes I did!"

Matilda turned to the other girls. "She never paid me, did she? You were watching. She never gave me nothing."

One girl looked as if she didn't know what to say. The others backed Matilda up. They stared at me as if I was a dog that had rolled in something disgusting.

Matilda said, "They're all the same, these foreigners. Trying to get in where they're not wanted. Now clear off. Get out of here!"

I had a bit more money, but I knew it wouldn't help me. If I handed it over, Matilda would do the same thing again.

What could I do? It was five against one. Joss had already gone in – I could see her talking to Kieran. Probably she wouldn't even miss me.

I walked away. All down the corridor I could hear them laughing.

Chapter 8:

The hospital

I was so angry, I felt as if I was burning up inside. *Get out*, she'd said – okay, I would! And I'd never go back!

I walked straight out the front gate of the school. At Mallenford, Year 7 pupils weren't allowed to leave during the lunch break, but at Tealbridge no one seemed to care.

Why did Matilda and her friends hate me? What had I ever done to them? They didn't even know me. Just because of the way I looked, they treated me like dirt. It wasn't fair!

I wanted to get back at them. I wanted to hurt them. But I felt powerless. I would never be able to make them feel rejected and despised, the way they'd made me feel.

Full of anger and pent-up energy, I walked for quite a long way. I didn't care where I was going, as long as it was away from school. At first I hardly noticed my surroundings. Then I began to think about how I would get back to Mallenford. The easiest way would be on the school bus at 3.30, so I'd better make sure I could find my way back to the bus stop.

I didn't know Tealbridge all that well. It was a bit of a dump, by the look of things. There were hardly any decent shops. I saw lots of charity shops, and several boarded-up shop fronts, although Tealbridge hadn't been nearly as badly flooded as Mallenford. It had been damaged in a different way – by litter and scribbled graffiti and years of neglect.

It was only 1.15 – ages until the bus would come. I wondered how to fill in the time. I didn't have enough money to sit in a café all afternoon.

Then I saw a sign pointing to the hospital. Tealbridge Hospital – wasn't that where they had taken the Chinese girl we rescued from the river? We'd never known what happened to her. I decided to make it my mission to find out.

I went first to the Accident and Emergency Department. That was the place where ambulances brought people, but at the moment things were quiet. When I explained what I wanted to know, the receptionist looked through the records on her computer.

"I think this might be the person you're talking about," she said. "An unnamed girl, brought in by ambulance on the day of the flood. She was admitted to Smeaton Ward."

"What happened to her?" I said.

"I can't tell you that because I don't have her name. The main hospital records are all filed by name."

"I'm not sure, but I think she might be called Leanne, or something like that."

"It's her last name that I need. But if you went along to the ward, they might be able to help you."

Following various signs, I found my way through a maze of corridors and stairways. I wondered how the Chinese girl had felt when she was brought to this huge building, full of strangers talking a strange language.

Whenever I tried to picture her face, I saw fear. She'd been afraid of the river, which wasn't surprising. But she'd also been frightened of Mum and me, and the medics, and the boatman. Frightened of everyone, in fact. Why?

At last I reached Smeaton Ward. A nurse at the desk looked up as I came in. "Visiting hour hasn't started yet," she said frostily.

"I'm not here to visit... I mean, I only came in to ask about someone," I said.

"Name?"

"Maya Grant. Oh... you mean the name of the girl I'm looking for."

"That would be helpful, yes."

"I think... I'm not sure... I think her name is something like Leanne. She looks like she could be Chinese. I just want to find out what happened to her."

"I see." Her cold, unfriendly gaze made me feel like an idiot. Worse than an idiot, a total nuisance, wasting her time with questions about a girl whose name I didn't even know.

"You're not a family member, are you?" the nurse said. "In that case I can't give you any information. Sorry." She didn't sound sorry in the slightest.

"Look, I'm not family or anything, but I did help to rescue her," I said. "Can't you even tell me if she's still alive?"

"She is alive. She was discharged from hospital yesterday. That's all I can tell you," the nurse said stiffly. She started sorting through a pile of papers, ignoring me.

I had come to a dead end. Oh well... I'd tried.

But as I walked down the corridor, someone called, "Wait a minute!" It was a middle-aged woman in a green overall marked *Hospital Hygiene Services*.

"That ward sister's a right cow," she said. "Don't let her get to you, love. *I* don't. Did you want to know about the mystery girl?"

I nodded.

The woman said, "We called her the mystery girl because she never said nothing. They tried all sorts – different people what knew different languages. There are lots of languages in China, did you know that? But maybe you're Chinese too. Are you her sister?"

I explained how I'd helped to pull the girl out of the river. "What happened to her after they brought her here?"

"She was quite ill for a few days, feverish like. There's an illness you can get from rat pee in rivers. But when she got better she still wasn't saying a word. They never even found out her name or how old she was."

"Did she have any visitors?" I asked.

"She did have one. But Sister threw him out."

"Why?"

"He upset the poor kid. He said he was a reporter from the *Herald*, but I bet he made that up, because when the girl saw his face she started screaming. Only sound I ever heard her make – a scream of terror. And Sister said, *I must ask you to leave. You're disturbing the patient.*"

"I wonder why she was so scared," I said. "Do you think she knew the man?"

"I reckon she did. And he looked like a nasty piece of work. Big, tough-looking chap, with a shaved head and a nose that looked like it got broke in a fight. I wouldn't want to meet him alone on a dark night!"

I said, "The ward sister told me the girl left yesterday. Do you know where she went?"

"Most likely she got took into care. I saw the hospital social worker talking to her, or trying to. Of course, he had no more luck than the rest of them. But that's what will have happened. The Social people will have put her in a home."

"In a home?" For a moment, I had a mental picture of a dogs' home, full of strays that nobody wanted.

"Yeah, a children's home. Don't you worry about her, love. I'm sure she'll be OK."

Another dead end... If I went to the town hall, or wherever it was that social workers operated from, I might be able to find out more. But time was getting on. I'd better try to find my way back to the school bus.

Although it had started raining, I was glad to get out of the hospital, with its smell of air freshener and boiled cabbage. And I wondered if the mystery girl had been glad to leave it, too. I was hoping that wherever she was now, it was somewhere nice, where she'd be well looked after.

Why wouldn't she speak? I knew she wasn't deaf or dumb because I'd heard her speak, just once. And I thought she'd understood my question in English, asking her name. But, of course, that didn't prove she spoke a lot of English. "What's your name?" is about the first thing they teach you in a foreign language. I had learned it in German and French, although I didn't know much else.

I was guessing the reason for her silence was pure fear. She was afraid to talk – afraid to give away anything about who she was and where she'd come from.

But why? And who was the mean-looking man who'd frightened her? As soon as she saw him she had started screaming – even before he said or did anything. He must be someone she already knew. Someone she had good reason to be afraid of.

By now it was raining hard. My hair was soaked. I didn't have a jacket or anything – it was still in school.

And I was a long way from the bus stop. Far in the distance, I could see the old-fashioned clock tower on top of the school.

I took what looked like a short cut down a deserted street alongside the railway. On one side was the railway embankment. On the other was a shut-down factory, covered in graffiti. Its name had once been TEALBRIDGE SINKS & BATHS, but a spray-can had changed this slightly. It now said TEALBRIDGE STINKS.

Suddenly, I heard the screech of brakes. I looked round. A car which had passed me, going in the opposite direction, had stopped suddenly.

It reversed until it was level with me. The driver, a youngish man, opened his window.

"Want a lift, kid? You look a bit wet."

I shook my head and walked on. I knew it was dumb to take lifts from strangers. Especially when they hadn't even been going the same way as I was.

The street was quite empty. Was I silly to feel frightened?

"It's her all right," I heard someone say.

Two men leapt out of the car. I started running, but they caught me before I'd gone ten yards.

One of them grabbed me and put his hand over my mouth. The other waved a knife in front of my face.

"Get in the car," said the first one. "And don't try anything stupid."

"You are in big trouble," the other one said, grinning. "Wait till the boss man sees you. You are going to wish you'd never been born."

Chapter 9:

They all look alike

They made me lie down on the floor in the back of the car. One of the men threw his jacket over me. He sat down with his feet resting on top of me, pressing me against the floor.

I was shaking with fear. Why had they captured me? What were they planning to do?

The car started moving. Hidden under the jacket, which smelled of sweat and cigarette smoke, I couldn't see a thing. But I could hear. It sounded as if one of them was talking on his phone.

"We got her," he said. "Yeah! In town, half a mile from the hospital. She was walking along the street quite casual like. So we grabbed her."

There was a pause, then he said, "Of course I'm sure! She's Chinese, ain't she? Okay, so they all look alike, but how many Chinky girls do you reckon there are in Tealbridge?"

It was starting to dawn on me what had happened. They thought I was the mystery girl! They must be totally thick. I didn't look much like her – especially not my hair. Her hair was dark and straight; mine was curly and reddish-brown. But then I remembered that my hair was soaking wet. Rain always made it look much straighter and darker.

"Look, I'm not who you think –" I tried to say.

"Shut up," the man growled, kicking me. "I got a knife. Understand? Knife. Cut you. So be quiet."

I was quiet.

He went on with his phone call. "Nah, nobody seen us, I guarantee it. Okay, see you in a bit."

"Was that Marie?" the other guy said.

"Yeah. She said to take the girl over there. The boss owes us a few drinks for this!"

We seemed to drive for quite a time. I couldn't tell what direction we were travelling in. After a while, the road felt bumpy, as if it was full of ruts and potholes. A farm track? And there was a strange smell, like meat that had started to go off... I felt my stomach heave.

A dog was barking fiercely. The car stopped, and I heard a woman's voice.

"Don't stop here," she ordered. "Drive into the garage and shut the door."

"Why?"

"Because I said so. Just do it!"

Next thing I knew, I was being pulled out of the car. That sick feeling came over me again. I coughed and retched, but nothing came up.

Everything around me was dark. Then someone shone a torch straight in my face. The others could see me, but I couldn't see them. I heard a sudden in-drawn breath.

"You idiots! You got the wrong girl!" The woman sounded furious.

"I tried to tell them," I said.

"Tried to tell them what?" Her voice was as sharp as a knife-blade.

"That I'm not... that I'm not who they thought I was." Somehow I knew it was better not to mention the Chinese girl. Better to pretend to know nothing at all. "Can I go now?"

Nobody answered that. There was a chilling silence.

"We can't just let her go," said one of the men. "She'll go straight to the cops."

"I won't," I said. I couldn't stop my voice from shaking. "I won't tell a soul, I promise. Let me go home... oh please..."

"Shut your face," a man said angrily.

"No, you shut your face," the woman told him. "I'm trying to think. How old are you, kid?"

"Twelve."

I tried to shade my eyes from the light that was shining into them. But someone grabbed my arms and held them tightly.

"She saw us. It was broad daylight," he said. "She saw the car, too."

"The boss would say get rid of her," the other man said.

The woman swore at him. "That would only make things worse. Her family will get worried if she suddenly disappears. They'll go to the police. You know what it's like when a kid goes missing – a huge search. And how do you know you didn't get caught on a CCTV camera?"

The men were silent.

"Oh, please let me go," I begged. "I won't say a word to anybody if you let me go."

"Let's see. What kind of a car was it that picked you up?" the woman asked me.

"I didn't notice. A grey car... not very big. That's all I know," I gabbled.

"And the men?"

"I didn't see them properly. It all happened so fast." That wasn't true. I was pretty sure I would know at least one of them again, the one with the knife. He had a thin, lopsided face, with one eyebrow slightly higher than the other. But the less I said, the better.

"What's your name, and where do you live?"

Should I answer that? I didn't want these people to know anything about me. I was so scared, I couldn't think straight.

"Your name, kid," growled the man who was holding my arms. He tightened his grip, and I cried out in pain.

All at once I heard my phone ringing. It was still in the car. If only I could get to it!

"Switch that phone off," the woman ordered. "Wait a minute. Did the kid have a school bag? Bring it here."

The torchlight moved onto my bag, as someone opened it and found the name written on the inside. Of course, like everything I was wearing, the bag wasn't really mine. June had found it for me in her attic.

A man said, "Here we go. Laura Robertson, 11 Valley Road, Mallenford. There's a phone number, too."

Shining the light on me again, the woman said, "Okay, Laura. Here's what we'll do. We'll let you go home. Isn't that kind of us?"

I nodded frantically.

"And in return, you won't tell anybody what happened to you today. All right? Because if you do... well, we know where you live. You don't want anything to happen to your family, do you?"

"No," I whispered.

"Or to yourself, of course. And nothing will happen, if you keep quiet."

"I will. I promise I will."

"If anyone asks why you're late home, say you were kept in at school, all right?" Then her voice, which had sounded almost friendly, suddenly became as hard as a fist. "And don't even think about going to the police. If you do, you'll really wish you hadn't."

* * *

They put a sack over my head and shoved me back into the car. I had to lie on the floor again. I heard doors creak open, and the car set off again out of the garage and along the rutted road.

After a while the two men started arguing about where to take me. In the end they decided on a wood near the edge of Mallenford.

"Yeah, it should be dark by the time we get there. And I can drive off the road a bit, into the trees."

"Don't stop if there's anyone around. Go on somewhere else."

"Do you think I'm stupid?"

"Well, it wasn't exactly a smart move, picking the girl up. Was it?"

"You're the one who said it was definitely her. This is your fault. You better hope the boss never gets to hear about it."

"Are you threatening me? Because if you open your big mouth, I'm warning you, I'll tell him about that Romanian girl..."

"Shut up. Remember we got company."

"You what?"

"The kid. She could be listening."

I heard a laugh. "Don't worry. Did you see her face? Scared to death. She won't give us any trouble."

It seemed to be taking a long time to get to Mallenford, but maybe they were driving around, trying to confuse me about where we'd come from. They needn't have bothered. My thoughts were already confused enough, and I was trying not to feel sick again.

At last we stopped. It felt as if the car was reversing for a short while over rough ground. Then it stopped again with the engine running.

"Get out, kid."

I still had the sack over my head, but I could tell it was dark outside. It was raining, and a cold wind was blowing.

"Stand there. Don't move. When we drive away you can take that sack off. Not before."

I heard the car drive off. When the sound had faded in the distance, I pulled off the sack. Afterwards, I thought I should have been quicker – I might have been able to get the number of the car. But at the time I was too frightened that they would look back and see me.

I found myself on a rough track among trees. Walking for a few yards in the direction the car had gone, I came to an unlit road. Low in the sky I could see a pale reddish glow that could be the lights of Mallenford.

There was nothing for it but to walk there. I couldn't ring anyone because I didn't have my phone.

Until that moment, scared as I was, I had managed not to cry. But now that the danger was almost over, I couldn't hold back the tears. Crying helplessly like a little kid, I started walking.

I was longing to be home. But home wasn't home any more, and even Dylan's house didn't feel safe now. I could still hear that woman's voice, like a recorded message playing over and over in my brain.

We know where you live. Remember... we know where you live.

Chapter 10:

Safe and sound?

There wasn't much traffic on the road. A few cars went past without slowing down, spraying me with icy water.

All at once I heard a car come screeching to a stop. Oh, no... not again...

But then I heard Mum's voice.

"Maya! Are you OK?"

She was getting out of the car. I ran to her and held onto her tightly.

"What on earth's the matter? Did you miss the bus? Have you walked all the way from Tealbridge? You silly girl. Why on earth didn't you ring me?"

"I've lost my phone," I sobbed.

"Surely they would have let you ring from the school? Isn't there a call box? Never mind. You're freezing... get into the car and get warmed up."

She got into the back of the car with me. Vince, who was driving, said, "Are you all right, love?"

I didn't have to answer, because Mum said, "She's walked all the way from Tealbridge. And she's soaking wet. Let's get her home."

"From Tealbridge! Must be a good five miles from here," said Vince.

"I didn't realise it was such a long way." I knew this sounded pretty dumb, but I couldn't help it. *Don't say a word to anyone...* "It's only about ten minutes on the bus."

Vince said, "The bus can go a bit faster than you can, girl!"

"I was really worried when you didn't come back at the usual time," Mum said. "Dylan told us you weren't on the bus after school. And your phone was switched off, and it was getting later and later. So Vince said he'd drive me to Tealbridge. We thought we'd find you at a bus stop, not walking home!"

She hugged me again.

"Another time, don't be afraid to call us," said Vince. "June would always come and pick you up, or I would, if I'm at home."

"Thanks," I whispered.

I leaned against Mum's shoulder, trying to relax. I should have been able to feel safe and happy. But that voice was always there at the back of my mind.

Don't tell... if you do, you'll wish you hadn't...

★ ★ ★

Over the next few days, I tried to forget what had happened. But that was impossible. Over and over again, I lived through the whole thing in my memory. I heard those angry voices. I felt the fear, sharp as an electric shock.

And I couldn't stop myself asking unanswerable questions. Who were those people? What was their connection with the Chinese girl? If they did manage to track her down, what would they do?

I longed to be able to talk to someone, but I didn't dare to. If I told Mum, she'd make me go to the police. It would be on the TV news. *Schoolgirl abducted in broad daylight. Did you see anything? Call this number...*

And then I would be in big trouble. The gang – I thought of them as a gang, because I knew there were at least four of them – might try to snatch me again. Or they might break into the house, maybe set fire to it while we were asleep... My thoughts got more and more frightening, and I started having terrible dreams.

Mum began to notice that something was wrong. The noises that I made in my sleep kept waking her up. She asked me if everything was all right at school.

"It's fine," I said.

Actually it wasn't that great. Matilda and her friends were still picking on me, but that was hardly worth worrying about. After you've been attacked by a shark, you don't care about a few flea-bites.

"You know when you lost your phone," Mum said, "did you actually lose it, or did somebody steal it?"

It was easy to lie about that. "I thought I left it in my locker, in the bag June gave me. But the locker door is a bit dodgy – sometimes it doesn't close properly. Somebody could have nicked the bag and the phone."

Mum looked at me closely. "Maya, if you were getting bullied at school, you'd tell me, wouldn't you? Or if you were in any sort of trouble?"

"Of course I would, Mum."

"It's just that you don't seem... well, you're not your normal happy self."

I said, "I'll be OK when things get sorted out at home. It's very nice here, and Vince and June are lovely, but..."

If we moved back home, I was thinking, the gang wouldn't know my address. They wouldn't be able to find me.

Mum sighed. "You're right, it will be good to get back home. Maybe next week, if the place has dried out by then. Or the week after."

She hadn't said any more about selling the shop. This was because there was still a lot to do before it was usable. She was around there most days while I was at school, and I helped her at the weekend.

It was starting to look better. The old fridges had been dumped in a skip, along with the rotting food out of the stockroom. The whole place had been disinfected. New glass had been put in to replace the broken windows. But the building still smelled damp and mouldy.

All the flooded shops now contained big machines called dehumidifiers. They hummed away by day and night, drying out the atmosphere, helping the walls and floors to dry out too. At night, when there were no workmen about, the street felt strangely quiet and empty. All you could hear was the eerie, high-pitched hum of the machines.

The street was empty because it led nowhere – or rather it led to where the Old Bridge used to be. The river level had dropped a bit, showing the tops of the bridge piers like a row of broken teeth. But there was still not much progress in building a replacement bridge. Mallenford was still cut in two.

Evie rang me now and then from the other side. Her family had decided to move back home, although there were no carpets on the floors and not much furniture downstairs.

"How's school?" I asked her.

"Pretty well back to normal. In other words, boring."

I wished my life was boring. Ever since the night of the flood, it had seemed more like a scary ride at a theme park – one of those river rides where you get swirled around, sprayed with water, and dropped down waterfalls – where you have no idea what's going to happen next.

Chapter 11:

Good out of bad

On Sunday morning, Mum told me she was going to church.

"Why?"

"Well, June asked me if I'd like to go, and it seemed rude to say no."

"Is everyone going?"

"Yes, I think so. Do you want to come too?"

"All right." I only said it because I didn't like the thought of being left alone in the house.

I had been to church a couple of times in my life – once for a wedding and once for a funeral. I was expecting a cold, echoing, high-roofed place, with solemn organ music and a choir. But this church service was held in a school hall, and the music made you want to dance, not fall asleep.

After the singing they showed a video. It was the story of a man called Joseph who lived long ago. He had 11 brothers, but he was his father's favourite, and his brothers got jealous. They hated him so much that they plotted to kill him. In the end they sold him as a slave.

He was taken to a distant country – Egypt. He worked hard for his new master, but then his master's wife got him into trouble. Although he hadn't done anything wrong, he was sent to prison.

He helped another prisoner by telling him the meaning of a dream. This man was a high-up servant of Pharaoh, the ruler of Egypt, and he could have helped Joseph. But when the man was released from prison, he forgot all about Joseph.

One night, Pharaoh had a dream which really bothered him. It was about seven fat cows and seven thin, hungry ones. The thin cows ate up the fat ones until there was nothing left of them. Pharaoh couldn't forget this dream. It must have a special meaning, but nobody could tell him what that was.

Then the servant remembered Joseph. And God told Joseph the meaning of the dream. There would be seven years of good harvests, followed by seven years of famine. During the good years, it would be wise to store up plenty of food to eat in the difficult years.

Pharaoh put Joseph in charge of doing this. And so, during the time of famine, the Egyptians had food to eat. But Joseph's brothers were starving in the land of Canaan. They came to Egypt to try and buy some grain.

Joseph knew who they were, although they didn't recognise him. He could have refused to help them. After all, they had sold him as a slave. But he said to them, *You meant to harm me, but God brought good out of what you did, and I was able to save many lives.*

* * *

After the video, a man gave a talk. Some pictures came up on a whiteboard... the aftermath of the floods, with devastated homes and ruined bridges.

"Did you find yourself asking, why did God let this happen? You weren't the only one! I felt quite angry with God, actually. Couldn't he have stopped the river from flooding?

"Then I read the story of Joseph. His whole life was a disaster area. Hated by his brothers... sold as a slave... put in prison... lonely, forgotten by everyone... But somehow he went on trusting in God.

"When bad things happen, we have a choice about how to react. We can get angry and bitter, and turn away from God. Or we can do the opposite – turn towards God, and trust him to bring good out of what happened."

And then there's a third choice, I thought to myself... not to believe in God at all. It's pure chance that rules the world. There is no God. People who believe in a loving Father God are just deluding themselves.

Did that include Vince and June? Were they wasting their lives, trying to obey a God who didn't exist?

Not exactly wasting their lives, I decided, because they seemed happy enough. Maybe it didn't matter what you believed as long as it made you happy.

* * *

Vince wasn't very happy that evening, though. He got a phone call cancelling some work that he'd been booked to do. He was a carpenter, and he'd planned to spend the next few days fitting a new kitchen. The last-minute cancellation had left him with no work for the week. And no work meant no money.

"Why did they cancel so suddenly?" June asked him.

"He said they'd decided not to do the work just yet. But I'm not sure that's true. Most likely they've found some Polish chap who'll do the work cheaper than me." He looked angry.

"Why would a Polish carpenter be cheaper?" Dylan asked him.

"Look, I've got nothing against these East European guys. Some of them are real hard workers," Vince said. "But some are working here illegally, without paying any taxes. The taxman doesn't know they exist. That means they'll do the job for less than what I can."

"But that's not fair!" I said.

Dylan said, "You could do the same thing, Vince. If you don't write down some of the jobs you do, the taxman will never know about them."

"Some people do that, but I don't. It's dishonest," said Vince. "And you get into big trouble if you're found out."

He sighed. "I was looking forward to that job. Indoors, nice and warm. Now I'll have to try and reschedule a roof I was going to do later on."

"If you can't do that, I know somebody else who needs some work done," said June. She was looking at Mum.

"I do need some new shelves in the shop," Mum said. "But I don't know when I'd be able to pay you."

This was how Vince came to work in our shop. He replaced some rotten floorboards and put up rows of smart-looking shelves. He even fixed the leak in the bathroom roof.

"Look, you can adjust these shelves to different heights," said Mum, showing them to me at the weekend.

"Why would you need to?"

"Well, I was thinking. Maybe I'll reopen the shop, but not selling health foods. The trouble is, most of the supermarkets do health foods now, and I can't compete with them. I might start up again as a bookseller."

"But there already is a bookshop in Mallenford," I said.

"There was, but it's closed down. The owner was near retiring age, and he couldn't face setting up again after the flood. He sold up to a fast food shop. So there's a space for a new bookshop."

I liked this idea. Books should be easier to cope with than food. You didn't need to keep them chilled, or chuck them out when they passed their "best before" date. (Mum and I were always eating food that was past its date, because Mum hated to throw things away.)

I said, "We could sell teas and coffees, too, like that bookshop in Lowfield. It would bring people in."

Mum laughed. "It would bring all your friends in for free drinks, you mean."

"So? I'd make sure they bought a book occasionally."

"You like the thought of a bookshop, then?"

I nodded.

She said, "Vince thought it was a good idea, too. I don't know how to thank him for all this. He did all the work for free, you know. I only had to pay for the wood."

"For free? How much would it normally cost?"

"Hundreds of pounds, I should think. He said he'd rather be working than sitting at home twiddling his thumbs. But I'll try and pay him back when I can."

She hesitated, then said, "I can't help thinking about what they said in church. You know... bad things happen, but God can turn them around."

"You mean it was bad for Vince, having that job cancelled, but good for us?" I thought this was a rather selfish way of looking at things.

"No, I meant the flood," said Mum. "I thought it was a disaster, putting us out of business. But it might mean a whole new start. Who knows?"

Chapter 12:

Slavery

We moved back into the flat that weekend. It felt very quiet, just Mum and me.

"You will come back and see us, won't you?" June said when we left.

I was sure we would keep in touch with them. They'd become good friends of ours, all three of them. And of course I would still see Dylan on the bus every day, but I didn't think I would be able to talk to him much. Joss would only start spreading rumours if I did.

At least I needn't be afraid of the gang now. They only had the address of Dylan's house. If I did tell Mum about what had happened... even if we went to the police... they wouldn't be able to find me.

Or maybe they would. They knew I lived in Mallenford. How many Chinese-looking girls were there in Mallenford? All they had to do would be to follow me home after school.

Perhaps I would never be free of this fear... those dreams...

★ ★ ★

One morning at the bus stop, Dylan came up to me.

"You know that Chinese girl that you rescued? We think we know where she is now," he said.

"Oh, really?"

"She's living with a foster family in Lowfield. June belongs to this support group for foster carers, and she knows the people who are looking after her. I mean, I don't know for certain, but it sounds like the same girl. She looks Chinese, and she never speaks."

"That could be her." I couldn't help feeling curious. "What will happen to her?"

"I don't know. Because she won't talk, or can't, nobody knows who she is or where she's from. She's with the foster family while the social workers try to decide what to do with her."

"Does she understand any English?"

"It seems she does, a bit. And living with a family, she's probably learning more all the time. Her foster mum told June that she may be dumb, but she's not stupid!"

"I wonder if I'd be allowed to go and see her," I said.

"Don't see why not," said Dylan. "I'll ask June to call her foster mum."

I was thinking that the girl, if she remembered being rescued from the river, might trust me a little bit – perhaps enough to talk to me? Then I could warn her about the gang, and let her know they were still on the lookout for her.

Dylan said, "She's scared to talk, that's what I think. Did you see that TV programme the other day, about illegal immigrants?"

"No."

"I only watched it because of what Vince said about people taking work away from him. But it was interesting. Did you know that there are gangs who smuggle people into the UK? People from poorer countries want to come here because they think they'll be able to earn a good living. But when they get here they find they're not much better than slaves."

"How come? Slavery's against the law."

"But if you're here illegally, it's like you're outside the law," Dylan said. "You can end up doing a terrible, badly-paid job. And you're in the power of the people who brought you over here. They tell you that you have to work for them, to pay them back for smuggling you into the country. And that could take years."

"You could run away, couldn't you?"

"You'd probably be afraid to. Remember you would have no passport and no money. You might not speak much English. You wouldn't know anyone in Britain, except the people you came with. And they'd have told you that you would go to prison if you got caught."

"You would probably wish you'd stayed at home," I said.

"Yes, but it would be too late. You'd be trapped."

Just then the bus arrived. All the way to school, I sat thinking about what Dylan had said.

Could the Chinese girl be an illegal immigrant? Was that why she was afraid to say anything? She thought she'd get into trouble and be sent to prison. Or else she was scared of the people she'd been working for.

I wondered what sort of work she'd had to do, and where she'd been when the floods rose up and swept her away.

The bit of fence that she'd clung onto – that might be a clue. Unfortunately, we had thrown it into the skip with all the other rubbish from the flood. Anyway, there was nothing special about it as far as I could remember. It was just a fence panel made of wooden slats, like you might see in dozens of gardens.

She must have come from somewhere upriver, but where? From the far side of town? From somewhere out in the country? Or even from Tealbridge?

I was thinking so hard, I nearly forgot to get up when the bus stopped.

"Maya's dreaming," I heard Joss say to Amelia. "It must be love," and they both giggled.

★ ★ ★

That evening, I told Mum what Dylan had said. She was very interested, and rang June to find out more. June called the foster carer in Lowfield, then rang us back.

"She's quite happy for us to call in and see the girl," Mum told me. "The poor kid never gets a visit, except from her social worker."

"Do you think she'll remember us from the day we rescued her?"

"I don't know," said Mum. "She was in a state of shock, remember. She may have forgotten the whole thing."

June said she would drive us over to Lowfield on Saturday. It was only a few miles away, but the journey seemed to take ages, because June was a very cautious driver. "Usually Vince does the driving," she said.

As we crept along at a steady 40, with a queue building up behind us, we talked about Dylan's theory. I was a bit surprised that Dylan hadn't come along to see the mystery girl.

"Oh, he wanted to," said June, "but we thought it might be a bit much for the poor girl. Mandy said she's so quiet and shy, you'd hardly know she's there. She likes helping Mandy look after her little boy, and that's the only time you'll ever see a smile on her face, Mandy said."

"Maybe Dylan was right," I said. "She's an illegal immigrant who's been badly treated."

Mum said, "Do you remember that terrible accident a few years ago, when about twenty Chinese immigrants were drowned? They were collecting cockles on some mud flats at night, and the tide came in, and they couldn't get ashore in time."

"I remember that," said June. "Somewhere up north, wasn't it? They were working for a gang of criminals who'd smuggled them into the country. They had to do as they were told because they owed money to the gang."

"And then there was that truck on the cross-Channel ferry," Mum said.

"What truck?" I asked.

"It was full of Chinese people. They'd been crammed into the back of the truck to smuggle them into England. But things went wrong – the truck got delayed, or something – and there wasn't enough air for them to breathe. They couldn't get out because the doors were locked. Nearly all of them died."

"Oh, how awful."

"I don't know how people can treat other human beings like that," said June. "Like animals. Like cattle."

Like slaves, I thought. The mystery girl was right to be afraid.

Chapter 13:

Mime games

It was the same girl. We recognised her immediately – and she knew us. She looked quite shocked for a moment. Then she gave us a small, shy smile. She got up from the floor where she'd been playing with a little boy and his toy train.

Mandy, the foster carer, said to her, "Do you remember these people, Anne? They helped to save you from the river."

The girl shook our hands very formally, with a little bow of the head. She said nothing.

The last time I'd seen her had been weeks ago, when she was lifted into the ambulance, looking pale and terrified. She seemed much better now. Her eyes had lost that hunted look. She wasn't quite so painfully thin; her face had filled out a bit. She was wearing some new clothes, jeans and a blue top.

"We wondered what had happened to you," Mum said. "I'm glad you are OK."

I said, "I went to the hospital to ask about you, but by that time you'd left." Would she understand words like "hospital"? Maybe she didn't understand a word of what we said. It was hard to tell.

"Anne, Anne! Play with Joe," the little boy said, trying to climb up her leg. She understood that all right. She picked him up and tickled him under the chin, making him laugh.

"How did you find out her name?" Mum asked Mandy.

"We didn't. It was the social worker who called her Anne – short for Anonymous."

"The funny thing is," I said, "I think her name might really be something like that." I turned to the girl. "Leanne. That's your name, isn't it?"

"That doesn't sound very Chinese," said Mandy.

"Depends how you spell it," said Mum.

"Are you Li An?" I asked her again, willing her to answer me.

She gave me a quick, sideways glance from under her fringe of dark hair. Then, silently, she nodded.

Mandy looked amazed. Mum said, "Maybe we should leave these two together for a while, and see what comes of it."

"Oh! Right. Come into the kitchen. I'll put the kettle on."

The women went out and closed the door, leaving Li An and me with the little boy.

There was a silence. I had no idea how to even begin to ask her what I wanted to know. And I didn't want to frighten her, but all the same, I ought to warn her...

Speaking slowly, I said, "A man came to see you, didn't he? When you were in hospital. A bad man. The boss of a gang?"

Her eyes never left my face. She nodded again.

"You were afraid of him? Don't worry – he doesn't know you're here. His men were looking for you, and they caught me instead. When they realised, they let me go."

Don't tell anyone... Li An didn't count, though. She already knew much more than I did about the gang. Anyway, I didn't think she had understood me. I'd spoken too quickly, or used words she didn't know. Better keep it plain and simple.

"Those men are still looking for you," I said. "You should go to the police. Tell them what happened... they'll catch the bad men."

She shook her head. Her lips were shut as tight as a locked door.

"If the bad men go to prison, they won't be able to hurt you..."

I stopped talking. I was getting nowhere. Anyway, if I was afraid to talk to the police, how much worse would it be for her? In a strange land, trying to speak a foreign language, all the time afraid that the police might arrest her... no wonder she didn't want to talk about what had happened.

Little Joe started wriggling in her arms. She put him down on the floor again and pushed his train around the track. It was obvious she was fond of him, and I wondered if she felt happy here, where people were kind to her.

But she wouldn't be able to stay here for ever. It was only temporary, June had told us. The social workers were still trying to decide what to do with her. Eventually, she would get moved on somewhere else, or sent back home – if they ever found out where her home was.

I thought I would try asking her something different.

"What kind of work were you doing before the flood?" Unsure if she understood me, I started using actions as well as words. "Were you picking fruit? Were you making clothes? Or cooking? Or cleaning?"

I've never been great at acting. My mime of scrubbing floors made her smile. But then she started doing some actions of her own, with quick hand movements, pulling and plucking at something. Then she seemed to be wrapping the thing up. I had no idea what she was doing.

"What is that thing?" I pointed to the imaginary object in front of her.

She flapped her arms like wings.

"A bird? You were doing something to a bird?"

She made those swift hand movements again. Anyone would have thought we were playing some kind of silly game, like charades or something.

At last I got it. "You were pulling feathers out of birds. What kind of birds... chickens? And then wrapping them up."

Another quick nod of the head.

"Where was this – in a factory? On a farm?"

But she couldn't or wouldn't tell me.

"Where do you come from, Li An?" I tried to think of some place names in China. All I could come up with was Beijing and Shanghai. And Hong Kong, if that was in China... I wasn't sure. None of these names brought any response from the girl.

It's very hard holding a one-sided conversation. Soon I gave up trying. We both ended up lying on the floor, playing with Joe.

* * *

After a while, Mum put her head around the door.

"Time we were going," she said. "June wants to get back."

I said goodbye to Li An and Joe. As we were leaving, Mandy came out to the car with us.

"Did you find out anything?" she asked me.

"Not much. Only that she's been working on a chicken farm or someplace."

"She shouldn't be doing work like that, not at her age," said June. "She should be in school."

"We don't actually know how old she is," Mandy said. "But you're right – she only looks about 14."

90

"Why hasn't anyone reported her as a missing person?" asked Mum.

Mandy said, "What the social worker thinks is, she's an illegal immigrant. The people she's working for might not care too much about her – they probably thought she got swept away and drowned."

No, they didn't, I thought to myself. They somehow knew she was in hospital, and the boss came looking for her. How did he know she survived?

Suddenly I had a nasty thought. The TV interview! Mum had talked about rescuing a girl from the river... a young girl who looked Chinese. The interview had been on the national news. Someone from the gang must have seen it! If I hadn't been so keen to be on TV, Li An would be much safer now.

What should I do? Be careful... don't say too much...

I said, "At the hospital, I was told a man had been to visit her. He said he was a reporter from the local paper. But Li An seemed to know him, and she was afraid – she started screaming. So the ward sister made him go away."

"You never told me this, Maya," said Mum. "Until today, I didn't even know you'd been to the hospital. When was that?"

"Oh, ages ago. I went in my lunch break at school."

She gave me an odd sort of look – hurt, almost. She didn't like me keeping secrets from her. What would she say if she found out about the big secret – about getting kidnapped?

"Why didn't you mention it before?" she asked.

I shrugged. "Didn't seem important. Anyway, you had a lot on your mind, sorting out the shop."

Mandy said, "I ought to let her social worker know about this."

"Do you know any more about it?" June asked me.

"Not really."

Mum asked, "Was the man English or Chinese?"

"English, I think... I'm not sure." I told them what the cleaning woman had said about him.

"Did you find out anything else?" Mum asked. "Think, Maya. Even little details might be useful."

"That's all I know! If anyone wants to find out more, they should ask at the hospital. Not the nurses – ask the cleaner."

I got into the car quickly, before they could ask me any more questions. I was starting to understand how Li An felt. Safer to keep quiet and give nothing away.

I should warn Mandy, though. Letting down the window, I said, "That man might still be looking for her. If we were able to find out where she is, he might, too. Be careful."

"I will," she said.

Chapter 14:

Feed the hungry

On Sunday, Mum said she was going to church again. I went with her, partly because I wanted to see Dylan. I was sure he would be full of questions, and I didn't want to have to answer them at the bus stop.

The Joss/Amelia gossip machine was already in action. Evie had called me to ask if I was really going out with Dylan Harvey, and was he as loopy as people said? I was glad Joss couldn't see Dylan sitting down next to me before the service began.

"June said you actually got the mystery girl to talk to you," he said.

"Not talk. She didn't say a word. But she did sort of answer some of the things I asked her."

I told him all about our strange conversation, if you could call it that.

"A chicken farm," he said thoughtfully. "There can't be that many of them around here. It would have to be near the river, too, for the girl to get washed away by the flood. Maybe I'll go for a bike ride with Luke, and see what we can find."

Luke was a friend of his, a red-haired boy in Year 8. I could just imagine the two of them riding up farm tracks and onto private property… going up the bumpy track which had jolted me in the car… meeting that woman or those men…

"Don't," I said. "These people are dangerous. Li An was dead scared of their boss. At least, I think that's who he was." I told him about the man who had visited the hospital.

"Big and tough-looking, shaved head, broken nose? He doesn't sound like a farmer," said Dylan.

"He said he was a reporter. But I don't think that was true. I think it was just a way of getting to see Li An."

"Maybe he's in a gang of people-smugglers," Dylan suggested. "And he wants to get the girl back in case she gives away details of the whole operation."

"He needn't worry about that. She's not talking. She's really frightened, Dylan."

I wished I could tell him what had happened to me. But that might just make him more determined to find out what was going on.

If only I could talk to someone! I hated carrying this secret around with me, hidden away like some kind of shameful disease. I longed to tell Mum about it. She sometimes looked at me as if she knew I was hiding something, and it made her feel sad. We'd always been so close.

My friendship with Evie wasn't like it used to be, either. I used to be able to tell her absolutely everything, but not any more. I didn't often call her these days because it was hard to have a proper conversation.

Evie would say, "Are you OK, Maya? You don't *sound* OK."

"I'm all right. You?"

I felt totally alone. There was no one that I could share the secret with, except Li An. And she was no help.

I wasn't really paying attention to the church service. I stood up and sat down when everyone else did, but my mind was far away.

Then, after a while, some words broke through into my thoughts. They sounded familiar somehow.

"… hungry and you gave me food, thirsty and you gave me water," the preacher was saying. "I was in prison and you came to me…Whatever you did to the least of my brothers, you did to me."

I recognised those words. They were on the poster in June's kitchen.

"This is the way Jesus told us to live," the preacher said. "Whenever we help someone else, whenever we give to someone who is needy, he sees what we do. And it's as if we are helping him. Because he counts the poor and needy, the sick and the prisoners, as his brothers.

"So don't lose any chances. Don't walk past people who need your help… always do what you can for them. As a Christian, if you show love to people, it marks you out as different from everyone else. Because most people don't bother to do this. They think of themselves first, and don't care too much about anyone else."

Dylan shifted restlessly in his seat. He had a sort of cynical look on his face.

When the service ended, I said to him, "Why do you come to church, Dylan?"

"Don't know really. I don't believe half of what they say. I suppose I just come to keep June happy."

I said, "You looked as if you wanted to argue with what the speaker was saying back then."

"Yeah, well, even in church I don't think many people do what he said. You know… helping people, feeding the hungry and all that."

"June and Vince do," I said.

"Yes, but is it because they're Christians, or are they just nice people? I think they would be kind and generous, even if they never went to church."

"So what does make somebody a Christian, then?"

"Vince or June would tell you better than I can. Or my mate Luke – he believes all that stuff."

June came up to us. "I can't tempt you to come to lunch with us, can I? We were expecting visitors, but their car's broken down, and we've got so much food…"

"You must have been listening to the sermon, June," I said. "Feed the hungry."

I knew it would be a nice meal, nicer than Mum would have time to cook. And I was right. We had roast beef and Yorkshire puddings, followed by lemon meringue pie. June explained that she'd been expecting her daughter Laura and her boyfriend for lunch. But their car had broken down and they were still in London.

"I'm a bit worried about Laura," June said.

"What's the matter?" Mum asked.

"Well, she's been getting some strange phone calls. It's my fault – I shouldn't have passed on her mobile number. But how was I to know? It was a woman's voice asking for Laura Robertson. I just assumed it was one of her friends."

My heart sank. "What kind of phone calls is she getting?"

"This woman saying, *Remember, don't tell anyone. We know where you live.* That's all. Then the phone goes dead."

Vince said, "Laura's got no idea what it's all about. At first she thought it was one of her friends being stupid. She tried ringing back, but of course they'd withheld the number."

"It's happened a few times now," said June. "She doesn't think it's a joke any more."

"Why doesn't she change her phone number?" asked Dylan.

"Because she would have to tell all her 2,000 closest friends," said Vince.

"It's not funny, dear," June said quite sharply. "I keep telling Laura she should go to the police. But she won't listen."

I felt a bit sorry for Laura. All the same, I was glad this was happening to her and not me. She was grown up – she could probably handle it.

But what would happen if that woman realised she'd got the wrong person? Would she try to find me?

"There are some nasty people in the world," June was saying. "Especially in London."

Not only in London, I wanted to tell her. Some of them are much closer to home.

Chapter 15:

The middle of nowhere

I got a new phone. My old one, luckily, had been insured against being lost or stolen. I'd had to carry on telling the story I'd told Mum about losing it at school. I could see she didn't quite believe me, but she didn't know what to do about it. This was a new situation – I'd hardly ever lied to her before.

Anyway, at the moment she was busy painting the shop, getting ready for the grand re-opening as a bookstore. She'd had to borrow a lot of money in order to buy books to sell. I knew she was worried about how to repay the money if the shop wasn't a success.

I helped with the painting as much as I could. It was half-term week, so I had plenty of time. The smell of new paint replaced the old, damp, mouldy smells, and the shop began to look really good.

Halfway through the week, I'd finished all the bits that I could paint. I was on the computer, trying to design a poster for the opening day, when Mum called up the stairs, "You've got visitors, Maya."

I was expecting to see Joss and Amelia – who else could it be? Then Dylan and his friend, Luke, came up the stairs. I wished the flat wasn't in such a mess, but the

99

boys didn't seem to notice. They looked excited about something.

"We think we've found the place where that Chinese girl was working," said Dylan. "Want to see it?"

"Dylan! I told you to keep away from those people! They're dangerous."

"Don't worry. The place was totally empty," said Luke. "It looked like it had been flooded out and then abandoned."

Dylan plugged his video camera into our computer. While he was trying to get a picture to come up, Luke explained that they'd gone biking along the valley between Mallenford and Tealbridge. Wherever they could, they'd followed tracks and side roads leading to the river.

Dylan said, "Look, this was a road near the river. You can see where there used to be a bridge, but it's gone." The camera panned around, showing fields littered with stones and dead trees, hedges full of plastic rubbish, and part of a broken bridge.

"Nothing there, so we went further on," said Luke. "Fast-forward it, Dylan."

Now I could see what looked like a tree-lined island in the river. The camera zoomed in. Between the trees I could make out some kind of shed or barn.

"We thought this was strange because it wasn't on the map," said Dylan.

"Not that strange. The building could have been put up after the map was made," I said.

"I'm not talking about the building. The whole *island* wasn't on the map. The river's changed its course, by the look of things. See, it used to loop around that bit of woodland, but now it's taken a short cut and made an island."

"It probably happened during the flood," said Luke.

"So we went to explore," Dylan said. "We had to cross a couple of fields to get there."

"Didn't anyone want to know what you were doing?" I asked nervously.

"No. It's pretty empty around there. Just fields and a few farmhouses. Anyway, we waded across the old part of the river, where it was only about knee-deep –"

"You're crazy," I said. "Wading in a river, in February?"

"It was pretty cold," he admitted. "And I nearly dropped the camera. But look what we found."

The video showed a large wooden shed with a corrugated metal roof. Beside it stood a couple of dilapidated caravans. The shed doors were half-open, and as the camera moved closer, I heard Dylan's voice say, "This place stinks!"

Inside the shed were some metal tables, a couple of machines, and a row of big white fridges. The floor was strewn with rubbish left by the floods.

Luke pointed to the computer screen. "You can see a line where the water level came up to on the fridges. It must have been pretty deep."

Meanwhile, his voice on the video was telling Dylan, "Don't open the fridge! If the power's been off since the flood, it'll be disgusting inside."

The camera moved around some more. Shelving, bins, plastic trays, a huge roll of cling-film stuff... then it zoomed in on a roll of labels on a shelf. I couldn't quite read the label. Something about chickens?

"Want a closer look? Here you are," said Dylan, pausing the video.

He took something out of his pocket. It was one of the labels, torn off the roll. There was a picture of a hen pecking happily in a farmyard, and the words: "LAKE MEADOWS FARM CHICKENS. Organic, free-range, eco-friendly, full of flavour!" There was no address, just a website name.

"We thought this was kind of weird," said Dylan. "I mean, there were no chickens anywhere around there as far as we could see."

Luke said, "Maybe some of them got drowned in the floods, but not all of them, surely? And why were they being packed and labelled in that shed in the middle of nowhere?"

"It didn't look too clean, either," said Dylan. "I wouldn't want to eat anything that came from there."

I examined the label. "Let me have a look at this website."

It was the sort of site that Mum had used to order food for the shop. There was a whole page about how their chickens were reared, allowed to roam free in the fields, not shut up in huge buildings without room to move. Of course, free range chickens cost more than intensively reared ones. You had to expect that.

The website gave a mobile phone number, but still no proper address. When we did a search on "Lake Meadows Farm", the only results were the website itself and a couple of farms in America.

"I bet there is no Lake Meadows Farm," I said. "And I bet these aren't free range chickens."

"What are they, then?" asked Luke. "Ostriches?"

"They're chickens that have been kept indoors all their lives, in the dark so they don't move around too much, all crammed together. Each bird has a space the size of an A4 page to stand up in."

I knew all this because Mum had told me. She never bought chickens unless they were free-range... or supposed to be. But she couldn't possibly visit farms and suppliers all around the country. She ordered stuff on the Internet and paid for it with her card, and a day or two later it would arrive by van. We might even have sold some Lake Meadows chickens ourselves.

"Isn't it kind of cruel, keeping chickens like that?" said Dylan. "Why do people do it?"

"Why do you think? Because it saves money," I said.

Luke said, "It would save even more if they used people like Li An to pluck the birds and wrap them up. We think there were several people living there in those caravans."

Dylan started the video again. It showed Luke opening the door of a caravan. Some water gushed out, and he jumped backwards.

The inside of the caravan looked horrible. The walls were all mouldy with damp, and there were some bowls of food on a table, also going mouldy.

I was trying to get my head around the boys' discovery. They'd probably found the place where Li An had been put to work. It wasn't a farm or a factory. It was just a big shed in the middle of nowhere.

What had happened to the other people working there? Perhaps they'd managed to get away when the river flooded. Perhaps they were still working for the gang.

"Where is this place?" I asked.

"About halfway between here and Tealbridge."

Was this where those two men had brought me in their car? The thought made me shiver.

No, this couldn't be the same place. Of course not – the car wouldn't have been able to drive to an island. The gang must have another base somewhere else.

"What we ought to do is find out who owns that bit of land," said Dylan. "I think there was a farm on the opposite side of the river… Wait a minute."

He played the last part of the video. From outside the shed, wheel tracks led to the edge of the river – the new course of the river, created by the flood. On the opposite side, above the flood line, the tracks could be seen again crossing a field. There seemed to be farm buildings in the distance.

"That's as far as we went," said Dylan. "The river was too deep to cross. We had to go back the way we came."

"I wonder how you could get to that farm," Luke said. "I suppose you could go up the valley to Tealbridge, cross the river and come back on the other side."

I was hardly listening. The farm… Was that the place? The place where a car had been driven into a dark garage, and I had nearly been sick with fear?

I had no idea. I just knew that I wasn't going within a mile of it. Not if I could help it.

Chapter 16:

Dead end

The next day, Dylan called me. He sounded fed up.

"We went to that farm, but we didn't find out much. And we had to ride miles to get there."

"Dylan, you shouldn't be doing this," I said. "I wish you'd just forget it."

"Why? It's a mystery, and I like mysteries," he said. "Anyway, don't you want to know what we found out? It wasn't much. We spoke to an old guy – he lives in the farmhouse a couple of fields away. He used to be a farmer, but he's retired, and he rents out his fields to other people."

"Don't tell me," I said. "He rented that land to a guy with a shaved head and a broken nose."

"No, to a woman. A Mrs Jones. She needed a field to keep her horses in, she told him. The horses never arrived, but she still paid her rent in cash every month."

"Didn't he notice what was going on there?" I asked.

"Well, he is a bit… what's the word? A bit doddery, June would call it. He walks with two sticks, and he's pretty deaf – we had to really shout at him. And he didn't know anything about the Jones woman, except that she paid her rent on time. That was all he cared about. He suddenly realised that he hadn't seen her since the flood, and he got annoyed. So we left."

"You didn't find out an address or anything." I felt relieved about that.

"No, and there are pages of Joneses in the phone book. Anyway, it probably isn't her real name."

I thought I knew the woman's first name – Marie. That was what one of the men had called her. But I couldn't tell Dylan that.

Luckily, he seemed to have reached a dead end. Maybe he would get bored and forget the whole thing.

★ ★ ★

Half-term was over. We still had to go to school in Tealbridge, although it might not be for too much longer. The temporary bridge across the river was starting to take shape. It was made of metal girders, not nearly as nice-looking as the old stone bridge.

I didn't care what it looked like. Soon I would be able to go back to my old school. And that would mean never seeing Matilda and her friends ever again.

Luckily for me, though, there was a new girl in the class. Her name was Paresha – she was Indian. Pretty soon, Matilda's gang started picking on her, instead of me.

"Filthy Paki."

"She stinks of curry. She's disgusting."

"We don't like your sort around here. Go back where you came from!"

I wondered if I should say something to a teacher. But I didn't have much confidence in the teachers at Tealbridge. Most of them were useless – they couldn't keep order in class. So I kept my head down. I didn't want Matilda to start on me again.

But she did, of course, one day when Paresha wasn't in school. Because I wasn't looking out for her, she caught me on the hop. At lunchtime, she tripped me up in the corridor, and I went sprawling on the floor. All her friends howled with laughter.

Then, through the laughter, I heard a voice I knew. It was Luke, and he sounded angry.

"What did you go and do that for? Here, get out of my way. Are you all right, Maya?"

He helped me up. Matilda and her friends watched us, grinning.

"Ooh! The Chinky girl's got a boyfriend!"

"I don't think much of him. Is he the best she could get?"

"Is *she* the best *he* could get, you mean?"

"Shut up," Luke said. "Leave her alone. What's she ever done to hurt you?"

Matilda faced up to him. She was slow and heavy, he was lean and fierce. It was like a hippo meeting a tiger.

"Why don't you get lost and mind your own business?" she said to him.

"I asked you a question," he said. "Why are you picking on somebody who never did anything to you?"

"Because she's a Chink, and I hate them! I hate all foreigners. Coming over here, taking our jobs! We should get rid of the lot of them!"

"Yeah, get rid of them!" another girl said. "Send them back where they came from."

Luke said, "Maya hasn't taken anybody's job! You're talking a load of rubbish."

"Oh yeah? You try saying that to my mum," Matilda said. "She lost her job because of a load of filthy Chinese – like her." She spat on the floor at my feet.

"Matilda Barnes!" said a steel-hard voice, and suddenly everything went quiet.

It was Miss Cary, the deputy head. She was the only teacher in Tealbridge who could cause a silence like that.

"Matilda, it seems you have some lessons to learn about basic hygiene. Clean that up, and then come to my office. The rest of you, go to your classes. That means now! Didn't you hear the bell?"

We went our separate ways. I was expecting Matilda's friends to have a go at me, but they didn't. And I wondered why Luke had helped me. He wasn't even a friend, not really.

Then some words came into my mind. *I was hungry and you gave me food...I was in prison and you came to me...* You could add to that, *I was being bullied and you stood up for me.*

Although I was grateful to Luke, I almost wished he hadn't got involved. It would probably just make things worse in the long run.

★ ★ ★

It did make things worse. But not in the way I thought.

At the bus stop that evening, I saw Luke telling Dylan what had happened. Dylan looked very interested.

"What did she mean about her mum losing her job because of some Chinese people?" he asked me.

"I have no idea. And if you think I'm going to ask Matilda – think again."

"I suppose I could ask her," Dylan said. "What does she look like, this Matilda?"

"Pig-ugly. She's the fattest girl in Year 7. Greasy hair, spotty face. She's horrible," I said.

He looked quite startled by the hatred in my voice. "Okay. I'm not going to ask her out, am I? I just want to find out where her mum used to work."

I hoped Matilda would tell him to get lost. But she must have been pleased that a Year 8 boy actually noticed her – because she answered his questions. He talked about it the next day, walking home with me from the bus stop.

"Matilda's mum used to work in a chicken factory. It wasn't the world's greatest job – but at least it was a job, she said. They had machines to take off most of the chicken feathers, but there were always some left, so she had to pluck out the last of them by hand, and then wrap up the chickens. There were about a dozen people working there. Then one day the boss told them they weren't needed any more. They found out he'd got some Chinese workers to replace them. Probably illegal immigrants who would work for peanuts."

"But that's against the law. Why didn't her mum report it?" I asked.

"Because she was afraid of the people she used to work for. If she got them in trouble, they'd get back at her somehow. And she had been breaking the law, too. She hadn't told the benefits people she was working, so she was still getting benefits that she shouldn't have been getting."

Luke said eagerly, "Did you get an address?"

"Tealbridge Chickens, in Eastfield Lane." Dylan was looking pleased with himself. "It's about a mile outside the town."

I said, "If these people already have a factory, why did they set up another base, the one you found?"

"Well," said Dylan, "I think you were right about them. They were selling off a load of ordinary chickens as organic, free range, expensive ones. Factories get inspected every now and then. They might have got found out."

"But nobody would inspect that hut by the river," said Luke. "And even if it did get discovered, there would be nothing to connect it with the Tealbridge factory. Very clever."

"I think we need to take a look at this factory place," Dylan said to Luke.

"No!" I said.

"You don't need to come with us, Maya," said Luke. "What are you so frightened about?"

When I didn't answer, Dylan said, "We'll ride over there on Saturday. I'll take the camera."

This was when I realised I couldn't keep the secret any longer. I was going to have to tell them everything.

Chapter 17:

Road closed

"You were kidnapped. That's a serious crime," said Luke. "Why didn't you tell the police?"

"Because I was petrified! Anyway, what could I tell them? I didn't have a clue where I'd been taken. I couldn't describe the car or anything. They'd never have been able to track down those men. And that woman said that if I told anyone, they... they knew where I lived."

"So that explains those phone calls to Laura!" Dylan said. "Scary. I don't blame you for keeping quiet, Maya. But now that we know more, I think you should go to the police. If they arrest the gang, you won't have to be afraid any more. And neither will Laura or Li An."

"What if we've got it wrong, though?" I said. "Maybe that chicken factory is nothing to do with the gang."

"What do you remember about the place they took you to?" asked Luke.

"Not much. Don't forget I was lying on the floor with my face covered up." I tried to relive what had happened – which wasn't difficult. I'd done that hundreds of times without wanting to.

"All I know is, we drove along a bumpy track... and a dog barked... and we went into a garage sort of place that was dark inside. Oh, and before that there was a sickly kind of smell. I can't describe it. It was a bit like meat that's started to go bad."

"Would you recognise it if you smelled it again?" Luke asked.

"Yes. Definitely."

Dylan said, "You could help us check up on the Tealbridge Chickens place – see if you think it fits what you just said. If it does, we'll go to the police."

"I don't want to go anywhere near the place! They might see me!"

"Look, we *won't* go near it. We'll just ride past without stopping. And you could disguise yourself, Maya."

"What do you mean? They're going to notice me even more if I ride past in a wig and a fake moustache!"

"Just wear something that hides your face a bit, like a hoodie. I could lend you one. We'll look like three boys out on a bike ride. Nobody will look twice at us."

Luke said, "Have you got a bike?"

"Yes, but I never ride it. It's probably all rusted up."

"Let's have a look."

My bike made them laugh. It was a girl's bike, bright pink under a coating of rust. They told me I would never get to Tealbridge on it, and Luke said he would borrow a bike from a friend of his.

Somehow, although I still didn't want to go, the decision had been made for me. I was going with them.

That night I had a bad dream again, the first time for days. I dreamed about being kidnapped, only this time the men were going to kill me. I ran and ran, through woods and streets and classrooms and hospital wards. But they were always behind me.

I woke up covered in sweat. It was a dream, I told myself. Only a dream.

Could dreams be a warning? I thought about that story I'd heard in church – the story of Joseph and Pharaoh's dreams. Maybe I should tell the boys I wasn't going with them. But I didn't want to let them down.

Mum looked rather anxious when I said I was going on a bike ride with Dylan and Luke.

"It's only to Tealbridge and back," I said. "We'll be back in a couple of hours."

Mum went on and on about the dangers of traffic, which was the least of my worries. But in the end she let me go.

* * *

The bike Luke had borrowed for me was a bit too big, even though he'd put the saddle right down. And I wasn't used to having to choose from 21 gears. But after riding up and down the street a few times, I began to get the hang of it.

We set out along the main road. It was a good day for a bike ride – bright and sunny. But I hadn't been on a bike for ages, and before long my legs were aching. I also felt much too hot wearing Dylan's hoodie, but I didn't want to take it off because it helped to hide my face.

I was glad when I saw Dylan signalling to turn off the main road. We must be nearly there.

I had imagined Eastfield Lane might be the bumpy track that I remembered, but it wasn't. It was a proper road. Maybe this wasn't the place… But then a hint of that smell came to me. It made me feel sick and faint.

The boys came back to see why I'd stopped.

"Are you okay, Maya?"

I said, "That smell… that's it…"

Dylan said, "Maybe all meat factories smell like that. We should check it out properly. It's not far – you can see it around the next corner."

"Stay here if you want," said Luke. "We'll go on and see what it's like."

But I didn't want to wait there by myself. I got going again.

Sure enough, around the next corner I could see the place. It looked very different from the shed by the river – two modern, warehouse-type buildings, surrounded by a high wire fence. *Tealbridge Chickens*, it said on the gates, which were closed. Inside was a parking area, big enough for delivery trucks, but empty. Of course, it was Saturday.

All the same, people were at work in there. A door was open, and as we rode past I could hear the whirr of machinery. Maybe the Chinese workers – if that was who they were – didn't get the weekend off.

"This isn't the place they brought me to," I said. I didn't know whether to feel sorry or relieved.

Dylan skidded to a stop. "But you recognised the smell. How can you be so sure this isn't it?"

"This place is right on the road," I said. "There's no track leading to it. And no dog, either. I definitely heard a dog bark."

"Wait a minute. What was that?" said Luke, listening.

We all heard it – a dog barking. The sound seemed to come from some farm buildings a little further along the road.

"Come on," said Dylan.

Luke could tell I didn't want to go on. He said, "We'll just ride past the farm and keep on going. It will only take a minute."

As we went past, I was almost afraid to turn my head and look. The farm was set back from the road... a rough track led to it... there were several barns and sheds – some without windows. And in the yard a dog was barking loudly. Everything fitted.

Any minute now, someone might come out to see what was upsetting the dog. I rode on quickly. A few yards further on, the road went into the cover of a wood, and we stopped.

"Well? See anything?" asked Dylan.

"That could be the place," I said rather shakily.

"The farm, not the factory, you mean?" said Luke.

"I suppose they could both be owned by the same people," Dylan said.

I said, "Everything about the farm looks right. And I could have smelt the factory from there."

"Are you sure about this?" Dylan asked. "Do you want to ride back and have another look?"

"No! I never want to go near that place again. Do we have to go back the same way?"

Dylan took out a map. After a minute he said, "If we keep on down Eastfield Lane, it sort of loops round into Tealbridge. Then we can go back home on the main road. It will take a bit longer, though."

"I don't care."

We rode a little way along the lane. But then we hit a problem... the river. There was a bridge, but it was blocked off with a barrier and a big red sign: ROAD CLOSED, BRIDGE UNSAFE FOR TRAFFIC.

"That probably means unsafe for cars, not bikes," said Luke.

"I don't know. It doesn't look too great, this bridge," said Dylan, leaning over the wall. "Look at that arch – there's a huge great crack in it."

He was right. The bridge was a single arch of stone and brick – the river here was narrower than at Mallenford. From the centre stone of the arch, a zigzag crack ran up towards the parapet. It looked as if it might fall apart anytime.

"Maybe we could wade across the river," I said. But then I thought again. The river looked dark and deep, flowing swiftly towards the edge of a weir a hundred yards downstream.

"No way," said Dylan. "I think we should go back the way we came."

I could see it was the sensible thing to do. But what would happen if those men saw me, right outside their base? And then there was the woman. I was almost more scared of the woman, although I didn't even know what she looked like.

"We'd better wait until it's quiet," I said.

"It is quiet. The dog's forgotten about us," said Luke.

"Let's go," said Dylan. "It will be okay, Maya. We'll be back on the main road in five minutes."

As we came to the edge of the wood, we heard the dog barking, and we stopped hurriedly. Looking through the trees, we could see a big white delivery truck bumping along the track to the farm. The driver opened his window and leaned out, yelling at the dog to shut up. It obeyed instantly.

I looked again at the driver... a big man with a shaved head and a bashed-in nose.

"That could be him," I breathed. "The boss man. The one Li An was afraid of."

"I wonder what he's got inside that truck?" Dylan said.

"Quick. Get the camera," said Luke.

Dylan snatched his camera out of the saddlebag. Looking around hurriedly, he chose a tree and climbed part-way up it. Meanwhile the truck was driving around the side of the farm buildings. It stopped, and the driver got down from the cab.

There was a hedge blocking our view. I could see the top of the rear doors opening – that was all. But Dylan could see perfectly. He started filming.

"People are getting out," he said. The dog was barking again – I struggled to hear him. "They were in the back of the truck. Ten… eleven… twelve of them. He's making them go into a barn."

"Do they look Chinese?" I asked.

"No. European, I'd say. Women and girls."

"We were right. He is a people-smuggler," said Luke. "What's happening now?"

"He's closing the doors. Oh-oh. He's looking this way…"

"Be careful, Dylan."

He slithered down the tree. "I think that man saw me! Maybe the sun shone on the camera lens. Let's get out of here!"

We grabbed our bikes. I struggled to get onto mine – the boys waited impatiently.

Then I heard a car engine roar into life. It came racing down the track from the farm and skidded to a stop, blocking the whole width of the lane. Two men got out.

"Hey! Give me that camera!" one of them shouted.

"Quick! Turn round. Go back the other way," gasped Dylan.

"But the bridge…" I said.

"We can cross it, they can't. It's our only chance! Get moving!"

Chapter 18:
The weir

We raced through the woods, heading back towards the bridge. Behind me, I could hear the car revving up again. I was going as fast as I could, but I couldn't keep up with the boys.

Dylan heaved his bike across the barrier and vaulted over. Luke was only a couple of seconds behind him.

"Come on, Maya!" Luke yelled.

I could hear the car getting closer. I reached the bridge ahead of it, though. The boys lifted my bike, and I scrambled over the barrier.

This wasn't going to save us. The men might not be able to drive over the bridge – but they could run over it. They could still catch up with us.

"Quick! Get going!" cried Dylan.

The road onto the bridge was uphill. I couldn't get up enough speed to get into the saddle. The boys had almost crossed the bridge – I was still hopping along beside the bike.

I looked back. The two men were climbing over the barrier. One was the big man from the truck. The other – I knew him instantly. He was the man who'd held a knife in front of my face.

He recognised me, too. "It's her! That Laura kid!"

"Get her," said the big man.

"You leave her alone!" shouted Luke. He came back over the bridge, riding at speed. Incredibly brave... but what could he do against men armed with knives?

Everything happened at once. The men ran towards me. I dropped the bike and started to run. Luke shouted something, but his words were drowned by a deep rumbling sound. The roadway trembled beneath my feet.

A wide split appeared right across the road, like a mouth opening.

"Get back!" someone yelled.

Too late. The bridge was falling apart underneath me. Roadway, walls, everything – falling, falling.

I fell too, helpless to save myself. And the river swallowed me up.

The water was cold – freezing cold. My whole body seemed to cry out in shock. Don't panic! Keep your mouth shut. Hold your breath.

I swam desperately, not even sure which way was up. All at once my head came out of the water. I took a huge, gasping breath.

Someone grabbed my arm. I tried to break free – then I saw that it was Luke. We were right in the middle of the river. My feet couldn't touch the bottom.

"Swim, Maya!" Luke cried. "Away from the weir!"

I tried to swim towards the bank. No chance – the river was too strong. It swept us along, faster, faster...

I took a deep breath and held it, as we went over the weir.

Water roared in my ears. The river pounded me and beat me. It was drowning me. I would never come up again…

But suddenly, my feet touched something solid. I managed to stand up. The foaming water below the weir was less than waist-deep. I was still alive – amazing!

Luke was right beside me. He grabbed my hand again. He began pulling me back towards the weir.

"What are you doing?" I gasped.

"Quickly! Get under here. Behind the waterfall."

"Are you crazy?"

"Those men. They'll be looking for us!"

Above us, an old supermarket trolley was caught on the edge. It made a gap in the smooth curve of water rushing over the lip of the weir. Luke pulled me through the gap and into a sort of cave. Water poured down in front of us. Behind was the wall of the weir. But in the long, narrow space between, there was air to breathe.

We were still waist-deep in freezing cold water. But at least nobody could see us here.

"Didn't those men fall into the river too?" I asked, shivering.

"I don't think so. They turned back just in time, before the bridge went."

"What about Dylan?"

"He was on the far side. They won't be able to get him... unless they've got a gun. If he's got any sense, he'll call the police."

"The police! But it could take ages for them to get here."

"Yes."

Luke was shivering, like me. How long would we be able to stay here before the cold got to us?

"Let's move along, closer to the bank," I said.

Keeping behind the curtain of falling water, we moved slowly sideways. We were heading for the far bank of the river, away from where the men were. Soon we had gone as far as we could. We were close to the riverbank – going closer would take us out into the open, in plain view of anyone on the other side.

Where were the men? They might think we'd been swept downriver. Or they might have seen us go into hiding, and waited for us to come out.

If they had guns on them, the riverbank wouldn't be safe at all. The only safe thing was to stay hidden. But I was so cold... I couldn't feel my feet...

"What should we do?" I whispered.

"I don't know."

His face was very pale. For a minute, he closed his eyes, and I thought he was about to faint. Then I realised that he was praying.

I prayed too. Oh God, help us! Show us what to do!

Luke turned to me. He said, "I'm going to take a look outside. If they shoot at me, stay hidden, all right?"

"No! Don't go out there. It's too risky, Luke!"

"Which is worse, getting shot at or freezing to death? Don't answer that."

He crept forwards, closer to the waterfall. I suddenly thought how brave he was. He had put his life at risk, all because of me. If he hadn't come back to try and help me, he would never have fallen into the river. And without his help I might be dead by now.

I was in danger and you risked your life for me…

I watched him slip through the curtain of water. Then he was gone.

Terrified, I held my breath, waiting to hear shouts or gunshots. But the roar of the weir drowned all other sounds.

Now I felt totally alone. If Luke didn't come back… if those men got him… nobody else in the world knew where I was. I would freeze to death here, and the river would wash me away. Lost for ever…

But he did come back. Not even the downpour of water could wipe the smile from his face.

"Come out, Maya! It's all right. Dylan says the men have gone."

"Are… are you sure?"

"Yes. And the police are on their way. We're safe now."

Chapter 19:

Out in the open

Luke helped me climb up onto the bank. I looked around anxiously. Upriver, I could see the broken bridge. There was no sign of the men or their car.

Dylan said, "They went back along the lane. They could see me using my phone – they must have known I was calling the police. The big man said something about getting the women out, and they drove off."

"Getting the women out? What did he mean?" asked Luke.

"I suppose he meant the illegal immigrants. He's probably loading them into that truck right now. But we've got the evidence on video. Are you all right, Maya?"

He'd suddenly noticed that my teeth were chattering. Out in the open, I felt even colder than in the river.

"Here, you can have my jacket. And you'd better start walking – it will warm you up a bit."

"Walking?" I said stupidly.

"Well, you can't ride. Your bike is at the bottom of the river."

We started walking along the lane. Before too long, we heard a car coming towards us. I had a sudden panic

– could it be those men again? Could they have driven around by way of Tealbridge, and come to get us?

But I needn't have worried. It was a police car. When the driver saw the state we were in, he told us we were going straight to Tealbridge Hospital.

All the way there, Dylan was talking non-stop.

"You came to the wrong side of the river," he said to the policemen. "Those men will be getting away in their truck."

"Don't you worry," said the driver. "We've got units going to the other side too. To the chicken factory, I heard somebody say – is that right?"

"Well, we think there are Chinese immigrants working there," said Dylan. "But it was the farm next door where the truck unloaded those women and girls. I don't understand that. Why would they be needed on a farm?"

The driver said, "That could be just a stopping-off place. Most likely they'll be taken to a city. That's where the big money is. There are criminal gangs making a fortune out of these people. They smuggle them in from Romania, the Ukraine, Nigeria, Thailand... all over the place."

The other policeman said, "Those women think they'll get good jobs over here. But more than likely they'll end up on the streets. Any money they get will go to the gang that brought them here."

"The gang kidnapped Maya, too," Dylan said. "But they let her go again. She was lucky. Tell them about it, Maya."

But I couldn't. I was too exhausted to talk, and too scared. I'd kept the secret all this time... How could I be sure it was safe to talk about it now?

★ ★ ★

June and Vince brought Mum to the hospital. By the time she got there, I was lying in bed with a drip in my arm. That terrible shivering had stopped. But I was still feeling afraid.

Had the gang been arrested? If so, it would be all right to tell the police about being kidnapped. But if they'd got away... I couldn't decide what to do. My thoughts went round and round endlessly, like a leaf caught in an eddy of the river.

It was good to see Mum.

"Oh, Maya! What on earth have you been doing? Are you okay?"

She couldn't hug me properly because of the tubes going into my arm. She sat down beside me, holding my hand.

"Tell me what's been happening," she said. "It started weeks ago, didn't it? I've known for ages that something was wrong. What is it?"

I found myself telling her the whole story. It was a relief to get it all out in the open.

She looked very angry. "Those men deserve to go to prison for a long time," she said. "And you could help to make sure it happens, by telling the police."

"But I'm scared, Mum..."

"Don't be. When they're locked up, they won't be a threat any more. But if you go on keeping their secret, you'll always be afraid of them... Can't you see?"

So the next day, I made a statement to the police. I had to tell them everything that happened the day I was kidnapped.

"Would you be able to identify those men if you saw them again?" the policewoman asked.

"One of them – yes, definitely. The one with the knife. I'm not sure about the other one. Did you arrest them, then?"

"We arrested several people at the farm yesterday. If you're willing, we can arrange for an identity parade. Do you know what that means? There will be half a dozen people lined up, and you'll have to point out the men who kidnapped you. Don't worry – they wouldn't be able to see you. You would be looking through a window with special one-way glass."

I really didn't want to do it. But as Mum said, it might help to make sure that the men went to prison.

"What about the woman, though?" I said. "I can't identify her... I never even saw her. All I know is that her name is Marie."

"Really?" The policewoman looked very interested. "That's the name of a woman we arrested at the farm. She keeps telling us she knew nothing about what her husband was doing. But this ties her in with it all right."

"Her husband – is that the big man they call the boss?"

"Yes. He runs the chicken factory. But he seems to have developed a profitable sideline. Every now and then he would ship a lorry-load of chickens across the Channel, and it would come back with a different cargo... people. We believe he was working for an international gang of criminals."

"Will he go to jail?"

"He's in prison now, awaiting trial. We've got enough evidence to put him away for several years. And the others too, with what you've just told me."

I said, "What will happen to the illegal immigrants?"

"I expect they'll be put on a plane back home. Some of them will be glad to go. Those Chinese workers had a terrible time. We interviewed one who spoke good English – she was a teacher, and she was told she could earn a decent living here, teaching Chinese. She thought she'd make a new life for herself and her daughter. But they ended up working an 18-hour day in a filthy shed. Then the floods came. The river burst its banks, and her daughter was swept away. She doesn't know if the girl is alive or dead."

Suddenly, I felt excited. "What was her daughter's name? There's a Chinese girl living in Lowfield. Her name's Li An, and I think she used to work for the boss man. We rescued her from the river on the day of the floods."

"That sounds like it could be the same girl. We'll have to look into it. Can you tell me her address?"

★ ★ ★

Three days later, we got a phone call from Mandy, the foster mum. The police had been in touch with her, asking her to take Li An to a place near Yanderton. It was a holding centre for immigrants and asylum seekers.

"There was a Chinese woman waiting to see us. And Li An cried out, and ran to her. Then they talked away in Chinese for ages. I didn't understand a word, but I could see how happy they were. I tell you, it brought tears to my eyes."

"What's going to happen to them?"

"I think they may be allowed to stay in England for a while, at least until the trial. Li An's mother is going to give evidence against that man. He was very cruel, she said."

"So the mystery girl isn't a mystery any more," I said. "Is she still with you?"

"No, she wanted to stay with her mother. Only natural... but little Joe is heartbroken. He keeps on asking where Anne is. I try to explain, but he doesn't understand."

I rang Dylan at once. I thought he would be pleased that the mystery was solved. But he sounded unusually quiet… depressed, almost.

"What's the matter, Dylan?"

He wouldn't tell me at first. Eventually, I got to the bottom of it.

"You know when those men were chasing you on the bridge, and Luke went back to help you? I know I should have gone too. But I didn't have the nerve."

I said, "It's a good thing you stayed where you were, actually. You were able to ring the police."

"No, you don't understand. I used to think I was much braver than Luke. He was always warning me not to do things – I would go ahead and do them anyway. But when it really mattered, he was braver than me."

"I know. He was awesome. And I never even said thank you."

As soon as Dylan rang off, I called Luke. I tried to thank him for what he'd done. He sounded embarrassed.

"You were pretty amazing," I said. "So brave."

This was the moment when, if I was a movie heroine, he would say, *I did it for you, Maya. I think I love you.* (Fade out to the sound of romantic music. The End.)

What he actually said was, "I didn't feel brave at all. Especially when we were hiding by the weir. But then…

you'll probably think this is stupid… I prayed for help, and I felt like I wasn't alone any more."

"I tried praying too," I said. "But I didn't feel any different. I was still dead scared."

Why did it work for Luke and not me? Why didn't God… if he existed… hear my prayer? It wasn't as if Luke was a specially good person. He was just a boy, an ordinary boy. Perhaps a bit braver than most.

Luke wanted to know about the identification parade. "How did it go? Did you pick out the men who kidnapped you?"

"Oh, yes. It was easy. I wasn't afraid because I could see them, but they couldn't see me."

That was kind of weird, I thought suddenly. It was the opposite of what had happened in the dark garage – when they shone a light in my face, and I couldn't see them.

Standing in the line-up, one of the men had looked rather nervous. (Serves you right, I thought… you're not nearly as scared as I was that day.) I was sure he was the man who'd been driving the car. The other, the one I called the knife man, stared straight ahead, as if daring anyone to challenge him. He had no way of knowing that on the other side of the glass, I'd already pointed him out.

"I may have to give evidence at their trial," I said. "But that won't be for ages. And they'll be kept in prison until the trial."

"Good. Do you feel safer now?"

"Yes. Most of the time I do."

I felt as if I'd just got off a scary ride at a theme park. You know the feeling – you can't quite believe that it's over. It nearly killed you, but it's over and you're walking away. And you wouldn't do it again for a million pounds.

Chapter 20:
The bridge

Mallenford was slowly recovering from the floods. Each week a few more shops reopened, although many were still boarded up.

One weekend, we had our grand Opening Day. A photographer came from the local paper, and a lot of customers arrived to look round. A few of them actually bought things.

"Business will get better when the bridge is open," Mum said. "At the moment, only half the town can reach us."

Work was going ahead on the replacement bridge. It was only a temporary structure, wide enough for one line of traffic at a time. But soon we would be able to get across to the other side of town for the first time since January. I'd be able to meet up with Evie and my other friends. And I could say goodbye to Tealbridge School… I couldn't wait to do that.

Matilda had stopped picking on me. Now she was trying to be all nice and friendly, which was almost as bad. It was because she knew Dylan was a friend of mine and she wanted him to ask her out.

I couldn't stand her. She was still being mean to Paresha, and once I nearly said something. But then, I changed my mind. No point in rocking the boat now… not when the trip was nearly over.

The last day of term was also our last day at Tealbridge. After Easter we would be able to go back to Mallenford School. Joss was quite upset on the bus home.

"I'll never see Kieran again," she wailed.

Amelia said, "What about me? Mr Gray said he was going to put one of my essays in for a national competition. But I bet he forgets all about it now."

I thought they were both idiots.

★ ★ ★

In the Easter holidays the shop got quite busy. Mum had taken up my idea of serving coffees, which meant that people stayed around longer and bought more books. At busy times, I helped her. I was trying to earn enough to pay for that borrowed bike which had fallen into the river.

One day a woman called in, asking for donations to the Mallenford Flood Fund.

"I can see you're getting back on your feet, and that's great," she said to Mum. "But lots of people are still struggling. Businesses have gone bust. People have lost their jobs. The people down Salmon Street lost everything they owned, and half of them weren't even insured."

I didn't see why we should give any money. After all, we were struggling too, trying to pay off our debts. But Mum was more generous than me. She wrote out a cheque, and afterwards she said to me, "I'll always remember how people helped us when we needed it. I want to give something back."

On Easter Sunday we went to church. It was a beautiful spring day. Sunlight streamed into the school hall, showing up the dusty wall bars and grubby mats. The music was even louder than usual, and people sang their hearts out, as if they had something to celebrate.

Weird, I thought. Wasn't Easter all about somebody dying? Okay, so Jesus came to life again... or so people said. But it was all a long time ago. Why were they still celebrating two thousand years later?

The talk began with a picture on the whiteboard: a broken bridge, with the river rushing through the gap.

"Do you ever feel that there's a gap between you and God? That you can't see him or know him, and he doesn't hear your prayers? There's a reason for that. God is perfect and holy, and we're not. All the wrong things we do, all our sins, have cut us off from him. The bridge is broken, and we can't get across."

Wait a minute, I wanted to say. I haven't done anything wrong. Other people have done wrong to me, but I'm innocent! I'm quite a good person actually.

Then, for some reason, a picture flashed across my mind. A ragged, hungry woman with a child… I seemed to recognise her. Oh yes, she was on the poster in June's kitchen. *I was hungry and you gave me food…*

But then some different words came into my head.

> *I was being bullied and you walked away.*
> *I loved you and you lied to me.*
> *I was living in fear and you kept quiet.*
> *I was needy and you didn't give me a penny.*
> *Whatever you did to the least of my brothers, you did to me.*

All right, God! Maybe I'm not such a good person. But most people are no better than me, are they?

"There are no secrets from God. He can see into our hearts," the speaker went on. "Even though we can't see him, he sees us and knows us. And he loves us. He hates it when sin separates us from him. That's why Jesus, his Son, came to earth. And the death of Jesus made a bridge across the gap… a strong bridge that will not break.

"We can cross the bridge if we choose to, by believing in Jesus and being sorry for the wrong we've done. But it's our choice. Many people don't want to make that choice, and then they wonder why God seems far away.

"They're right. He is far away. But we can cross the bridge that will take us closer to him. Any of us can do it, no matter what we've done wrong. And then we'll be on God's side of the river. We can pray to him and know that he hears us. We can trust him. We'll find that when bad things happen, he can bring good out of them, because he loves us.

"If you would like to cross the bridge, all you have to do is pray this prayer.

"Dear Lord, I'm sorry for the wrong things in my life. Please forgive me. I want to be on your side from now on. I want to know you and follow you. Amen."

There was a moment of silence. I felt as if I was standing on the edge of something. I had a choice to make – cross the bridge or stop on the bank? Give my life to God or stay in charge of it myself?

Taking a deep breath, I made my choice. I prayed the prayer and stepped onto the bridge.

★ ★ ★

After that day, my life began to change. It was Mum who noticed it first.

"You're looking so much happier," she said to me. "Are you glad to have got that secret off your chest? I wish you'd told me straight away."

"I know, Mum. That's what I should have done. I'll definitely do it next time I get kidnapped."

She was right – I was happier. Not just because I'd stopped being afraid, but also because I was learning the truth of what the preacher had said. I could pray to God and get to know him. I could trust him, like Luke did.

Evie noticed a difference too. No more secrets cutting me off from other people... I could talk to her properly and tell her what had happened.

She wanted to know all the details. Then she said, "I knew something was the matter. But I thought you'd made all these new friends at Tealbridge, and didn't want to know me."

"No way," I said. "I mostly made enemies, not friends. But hey... did you hear the bridge is opening on Saturday?"

"Yes! I can visit your new shop!"

"We can see a movie."

"We can go to the pizza place. Or the sports centre."

"We can go everywhere! Total freedom!"

She said, "My mum says it will be like the Berlin Wall coming down. Whatever that means."

I knew what it meant. Two halves of a divided town coming together again. Friends meeting face to face. Life getting back to normal, the same as it always was... or not the same. Maybe even better.

★ ★ ★

On Saturday, Dylan and Luke called in on their way to the newly opened bridge. I went out with them to take a look at it.

The bridge still had an unfinished look because it was only temporary. Already work had started on a permanent replacement for the New Bridge. When that was ready, the temporary bridge would be removed and the Old Bridge rebuilt, stronger than before.

"Crazy," I said. "That means the New Bridge will be older than the Old Bridge. They ought to rename them. Like the New Old Bridge and the New New Bridge…"

"Or the Old New Bridge and the Old Old Bridge," said Luke.

Dylan groaned. "Don't try to confuse me. It's a bridge – that's what matters."

We joined the crowd of people crossing the river for the first time in weeks. Halfway over, I stopped to look down, as I used to when I was just a kid.

There hadn't been much rain lately. The water level was low. The river ran smooth and gentle over the rocks, looking quite harmless, like an old, toothless lion in a cage. But I would never again think of it as harmless and tame. The river was wild – it could rage and roar. It could even kill you.

"Are you doing anything this afternoon, Maya?" asked Luke. "Because we've got a plan."

Dylan said, "Vince was talking about this place he used to go to when he was a boy. It's like a sort of fort, halfway between here and the sea. It was built during the war, when the Germans were threatening to invade."

"He says it's all overgrown now, deep in the woods," said Luke. "We're going to see if we can find it. You can come with us if you want."

"Vince says there are caves that go right into the hill. It sounds quite spooky." Dylan liked the thought of it, I could tell. "Dark tunnels... cobwebs... bats... dead things and ghosts and creatures of the night..."

A shiver of fear went through me... not terror like before – more like the sort of scary feeling you get before a fairground ride. I knew what real terror was, because it had haunted me for ages. But now I was free from all that. Free to go anywhere and do anything.

"Don't let Dylan scare you, Maya," said Luke. "It won't really be full of ghosts and things. Anyway, Vince is coming with us."

"I'm not afraid!" I said. "I'm up for it. Just give me a call when you're ready to go."